UNOFFICIAL

MINECRAFTERS

MASTER BUILDER

WORKSHOP

MEGAN MILLER

SCHOLASTIC

This book is not authorized or sponsored by Microsoft Corporation, Mojang AB, Notch Development AB, or any other person or entity owning or controlling rights in the Minecraft name, trademark, or copyrights.

Scholastic Australia
PO Box 579 Gosford NSW 2250
ABN 11 000 614 577
www.scholastic.com.au

Part of the Scholastic Group
Sydney • Auckland • New York • Toronto • London • Mexico City
• New Delhi • Hong Kong • Buenos Aires • Puerto Rico

First published by Skyhorse Publishing Inc, USA in 2017.
This edition published under licence by Scholastic Australia Pty Limited in 2024.

Cover design by Brian Peterson.

ISBN: 978-1-76152-767-8

Printed in China by RR Donnelley.

Scholastic Australia's policy, in association with RR Donnelley, is to use papers that are renewable and made efficiently from wood from responsibly managed sources, so as to minimise its environmental footprint.

24 25 26 27 28 / 2

CONTENTS

Introduction	1
1. Lighthouse	2
2. Hot Air Balloon	16
3. Ziggurat	19
4. Hedge Maze	31
5. Windmill	37
6. Pumpkin House	43
7. Market Stalls	48
8. Giant Water Slide	51
9. Rocket Ship	56
10. Mars Habitat	61
11. Pixel Art Diamond Pick	70
12. Massive Creeper	74
13. Cupcake Bakery	78
14. Haunted House	83
15. Secret Wishing Well	92
16. Car	98
17. Gingerbread House	102
18. Fountain	106
19. Jungle Tree Hideaway	112
20. Pigsty	117
21. Barn	122
22. Little Red Schoolhouse	129
23. Christmas Tree	138
24. Bridge	141
25. Cozy Castle	146

INTRODUCTION

I hope you have as much fun making these builds as I had creating them. They are small enough that you should be able to build them in Survival mode. You can follow these designs exactly or use them as a base for creating something completely your own. I've included tips for which blocks you can substitute, but really, this is Minecraft. You can sub in whatever blocks you like! With most builds, I've left the landscaping and interior design (and lighting—don't forget the lighting!) up to you. I'd love to see what you build, so if you want to share, you (or a parent) can tweet me at @meganfmiller. Happy building!

—Megan Miller

1. LIGHTHOUSE

Lighthouses were created to warn ships at sea of dangerous rocks or help guide ships to a town's harbor.

Lighthouses come in many styles and sizes. Often they were painted all white or with wide stripes to make them easy to see. They all have a source of light at the top to shine out to sea. We will first build the lighthouse tower itself, then the lighthouse keeper's cottage.

MATERIALS*

8½ stacks red concrete
7½ stacks white concrete
3 stacks spruce planks
2 stacks cobblestone
9 cobblestone stairs
12 spruce stairs
2 spruce slabs
3 spruce doors
24 glass blocks
36 glass panes
32 Nether brick fences
19 ladders
4 glowstone blocks
1 stone brick
4 wool, any color

*These material counts are based on the finished structure by itself, and the counts for the main blocks are rounded up into half stacks. Also, with this build and most others, we first create the structure out of the main blocks. (Here, the main blocks are red and white concrete and cobblestone.) Then we replace some of these main blocks with blocks used for windows, doors, and other details. This means you may need a little extra of the main building blocks to use only while building. You may also have some blocks left over.

Substitutions: You can use white wool and red wool instead of white and red concrete. You can also use different types of wood for the fences, wood slabs, stairs, doors, and planks.

1

This rocky promontory looks perfect for the lighthouse. A promontory is a raised piece of land that juts out into a body of water.

We'll need to flatten it out though. It's a lot of stone to remove, so I've used a little TNT before flattening the lot.

Clear out or create a flat area on land by the ocean that is about 30 blocks long by 20 blocks wide. The building itself has a footprint of 20 blocks long and 11 blocks wide. Along with this space, you will want a little space on the sides of the building and enough space to access the cottage door. Your building lot can jut out into the ocean. Just be sure that you position the lot so that you can easily get into the cottage from the mainland.

2

Here is the cleared lot, ready for building. I've placed 4 wool blocks to show the size of the lot.

Place temporary blocks to show the corners of the 20x11-block lot you will need. This will show where the building will go so you can see the space it will take up on your cleared lot. If you like the position, go to step 3. If you don't, move the markers until you are happy with the position.

3

The cobble circle is 11 blocks wide. Each "side" is 5 blocks long, and each "corner" is made from 2 diagonal blocks.

At the end of the lot, build a cobblestone circle—a Minecraft "circle"! The circle is 11 blocks wide and long. Its 4 sides are each 5 blocks long and connect to each other with 2 diagonal blocks, as you can see in the picture.

Place a strip of cobblestone a single block wide along the inside edge of this circle.

Now fill the interior of the circle with spruce planks to create the ground floor of the tower.

On top of the cobblestone-and-spruce layer, create a second circle—the same size as the circle you built in step 3—using white concrete blocks.

Add 5 more layers to this circle. (Each layer is a block high.) The first 2 layers should use white concrete blocks, and the last three should use red concrete blocks.

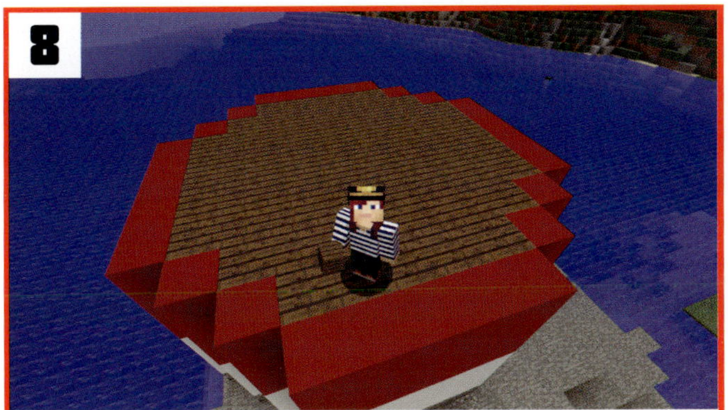

Fill the interior of the top layer of red concrete with spruce planks to create the second floor.

Now let's create a slightly smaller circle for the next level. The sides of the circle are still 5 blocks long, but they are moved 1 block in toward the tower's center. Instead of using 2 diagonal blocks as corners, use only 1 diagonal block.

Add 2 more layers of white concrete on top of this circle and three layers of red concrete. Fill the interior of the top red concrete circle with spruce planks to create the third floor of the lighthouse.

Now create another slightly smaller circle of white concrete. The sides of the circle are still 5 blocks long, but they are moved 1 block in toward the tower's center. There is a single empty block space at each corner.

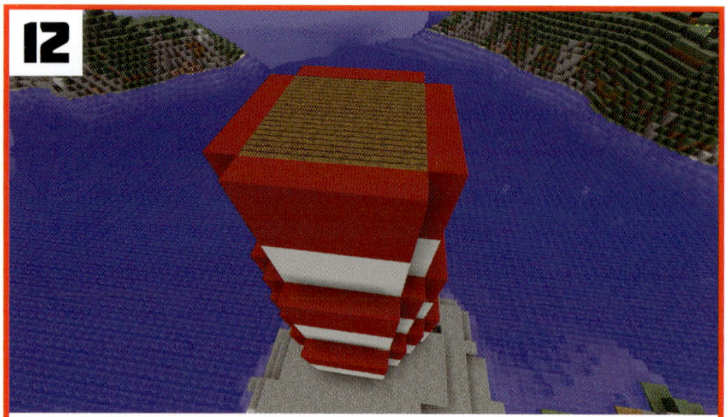

On top of this layer, place 2 more layers of white concrete and three of red concrete. Fill the interior of the top circle of red concrete with spruce planks to make the fourth floor.

The final set of 6 layers, 3 white and 3 red, uses a 5x5 square. Its sides are inset 1 block in from the previous set of layers. Use white concrete blocks for the first layer.

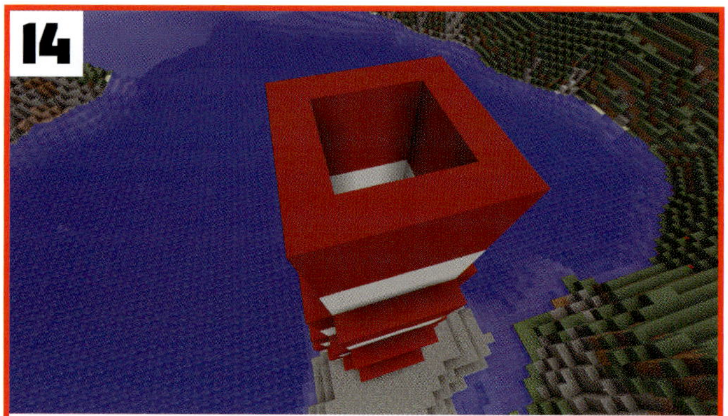

Above the first layer, place 2 more layers of white concrete and 3 layers of red concrete.

These four sets of red and white layers are the tower of the lighthouse. Now we'll build the gallery deck and the upper lantern room. Create the first layer of the gallery deck by using white concrete blocks to build a filled-in circle that is the same size as the circle in step 11. Each side is 5 blocks long, and at each corner is an empty space.

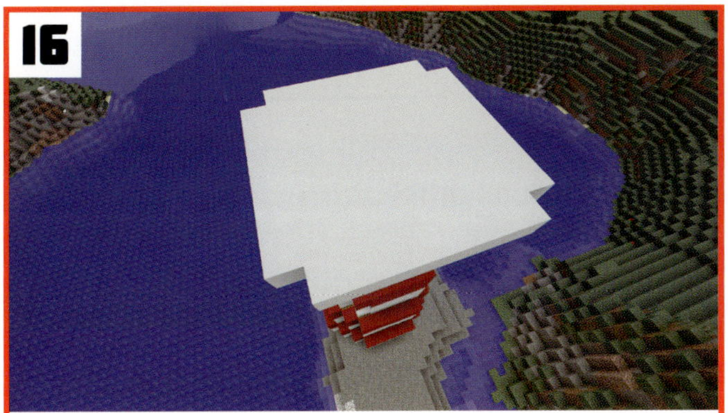

The next layer of the gallery deck is the same shape as the layer in step 15, but the sides are 7 blocks long. It extends 1 block further out than the layer beneath.

Place Netherbrick fences along the outside of the platform.

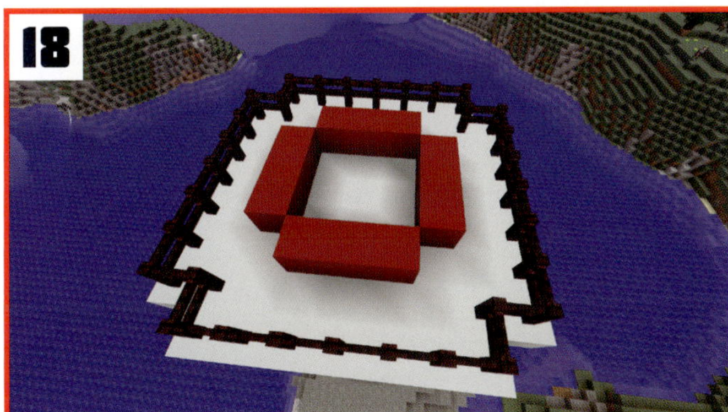

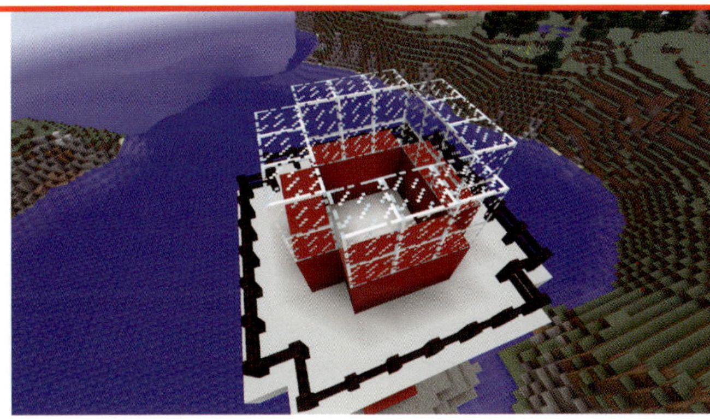

On top of the gallery deck platform you created in step 16, build a Minecraft "circle" that is 3 blocks a side (with a space for corners) using 2 layers of red concrete and 2 layers of glass. This is the lantern room.

On one side of the lantern room, knock 2 of the red concrete blocks out to make space for a door, then place a door.

Replace the 9 white concrete blocks of the floor inside the lantern room with spruce planks. Create the lantern in the center of the lantern room by placing a block of stone brick and topping it with 3 glowstone blocks.

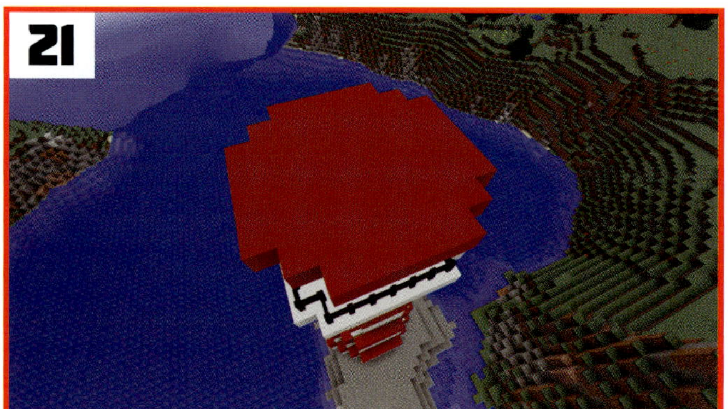

For the roof of the lantern room, use red concrete to create 4 more layers of Minecraft "circles." The first layer extends 2 blocks out from the top layer of the lantern room. It is a Minecraft circle with sides that are 5 blocks long and have a single diagonal block for each corner.

The second layer is a Minecraft circle with sides that are 5 blocks long and have an empty space for the corners.

The third layer is a Minecraft circle with sides that are 3 blocks long and have empty-space corners.

The fourth layer is a cross shape made with 5 blocks.

GETTING GLOWSTONE

If you are playing in Survival mode and you don't want to go to the Nether for glowstone, you can trade with a purple-clothed cleric villager for it.

At the very top of the roof, place a single block of glowstone. Except for details like windows, the tower is done!

Place the 7 blocks of the cottage width against the front of the lighthouse tower. This will leave an empty nook at the two back corners. Fill each in with a cobble block.

Now let's build the lighthouse cottage, starting with the floor. Along the front of the tower, build a cobblestone square that is 7 blocks wide and 6 blocks long. Add 2 blocks of cobble at the space remaining between the tower and the cottage floor, as shown.

Inside the square, add strips of cobblestone 1 block wide along the 2 sides and the front. Then fill in the center with spruce planks.

Build up the walls of the cottage with 4 layers of white concrete blocks. Leave 2 blocks empty in the center of the front wall and place a door there.

29

On top of the front wall of the cottage, build a triangle with 9 white concrete blocks, as shown.

30

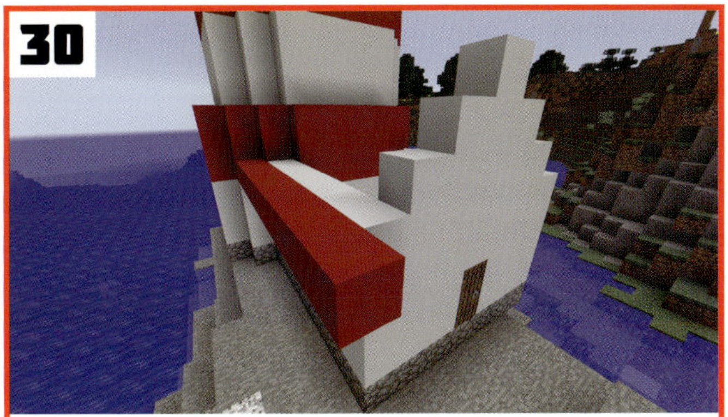

Now build the roof using red concrete blocks. Start with a row of blocks on the outer edge of one of the cottage's side walls. Place the blocks all the way back to the lighthouse. The row should also stick out 1 block from the front wall of the cottage.

31

With each step up on the white triangle, create a row of red concrete blocks that extends back to the lighthouse and 1 block out from the white front wall. Inside the cottage, fill in the central empty row in the roof with red concrete.

32

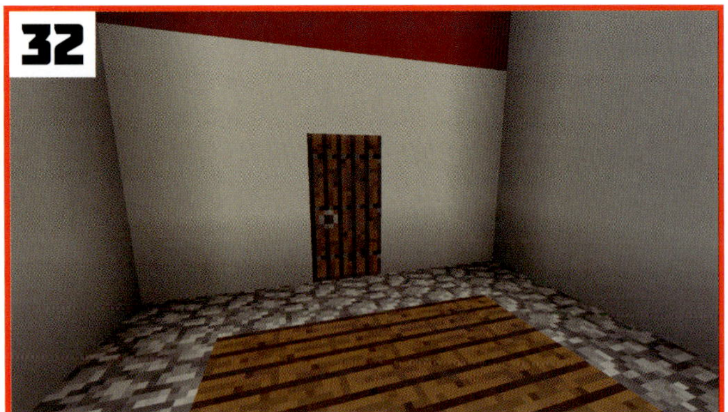

Inside the cottage, on the back wall, break 2 blocks and place a door to get into the lighthouse tower.

33

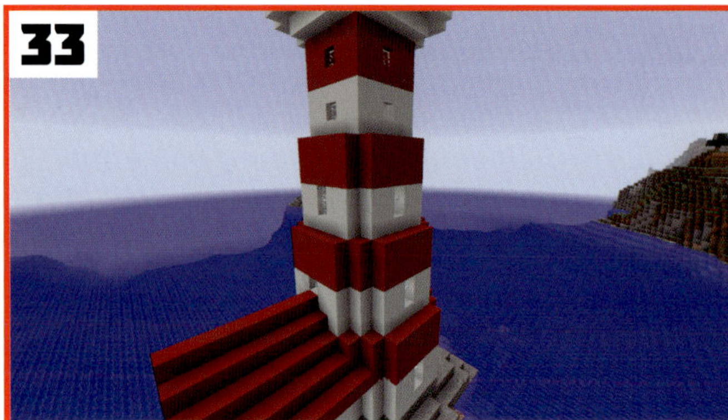

Now let's add windows. For the bottom 3 white layers, place windows that are 2 glass panes high on each side of the tower. (For the front of the tower, you will need to leave out the bottom window. For the second white layer, you can make a window one pane high.) On the top white layer and the top red layer, place a single-pane window in the center of each wall.

34

On each of the 2 side walls of the cottage, create a 2-block-high glass window. Use a spruce planks block for the bottom frame.

35

On the front wall of the cottage, on either side of the door, place single-pane windows. For the window frame, place a spruce stair at the top of each window and an upside-down spruce stair at the bottom of each. Two blocks down from the top of the roof, place a single-pane window. Above this place a spruce stair as the top window frame.

36

Add a porch to the front door. Make a 3x2 cobblestone rectangle with spruce stairs along each side and a cobble stairs at each of the front corners.

37

Add a porch roof. Place a spruce plank block directly above the door. Then put a spruce slab on either side.

38

The last task is to create a way to get up to each floor! Lighthouses typically have a spiral staircase running along the inside walls of the tower. However, with Minecraft blocks and a tower that gets smaller and smaller, this is very difficult. I've created a staircase to reach the second floor. At the very top of the staircase, I've used 2 stairs at either side to reach the floor.

39

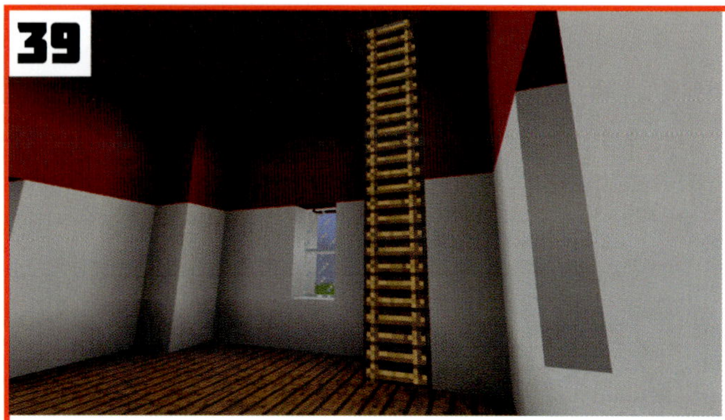

Ladder to the third floor.

Ladder to the fourth floor.

Place ladders to get to each higher floor. Because each higher floor is smaller than the last, place the ladders on columns of spruce planks that are inset 1 block from the side wall.

Ladder to the lamp room.

40

Now make the lighthouse your own! Decide what you want to use each room for and decorate it how you like. Outside, I've added a path made of bricks, granite (to look like crumbling brick), and gravel. I've added a little grass and some leaves as bushes. Inside, I used the cottage area for important storage while keeping the ground floor of the tower for a sleeping area and an entrance to a mining area deep underground. The second floor I've used for potion brewing, and the third floor is perfect for an enchanting station. The fourth floor is very small but has enough space for chests holding less important stuff.

2. HOT AIR BALLOON

The hot air balloon is the first recorded method humankind used to take to the air.

The first one was built in Paris, France, in 1783! Although today hot air balloons can come in many shapes, the traditional shape is this inverted (upside-down) tear shape. These balloons rise in the air because the hot air is less dense than regular air. In less dense gases, the molecules are farther apart from each other. Less dense gases (hot air) rise above denser gases (colder air).

MATERIALS

3½ stacks red wool
3 stacks purple wool
2 stacks orange wool
16 Nether brick fences

Substitutions: Use any colors you like for the stripes! You can also use cement blocks in place of wool and different types of wood for the ropes.

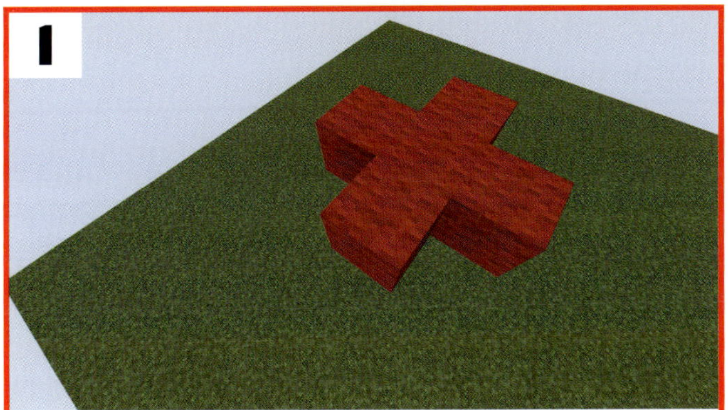

Once you've cleared the area for your balloon, decide how high above the ground the basket should be. In these pictures, my basket is 4 blocks above the ground, with 3 blocks between it and the ground. Once the height is set, place 4 red wool in a cross shape for the bottom of the basket.

Place 8 red wool above this in a square to finish the basket.

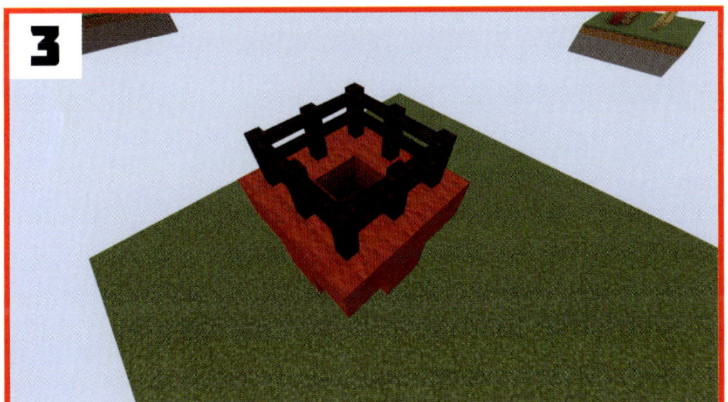

Place Netherbrick fence in a square above the red wool.

At each corner, place 2 additional Netherbrick fences on top of each other to create the ropes that hold the balloon to the basket.

5

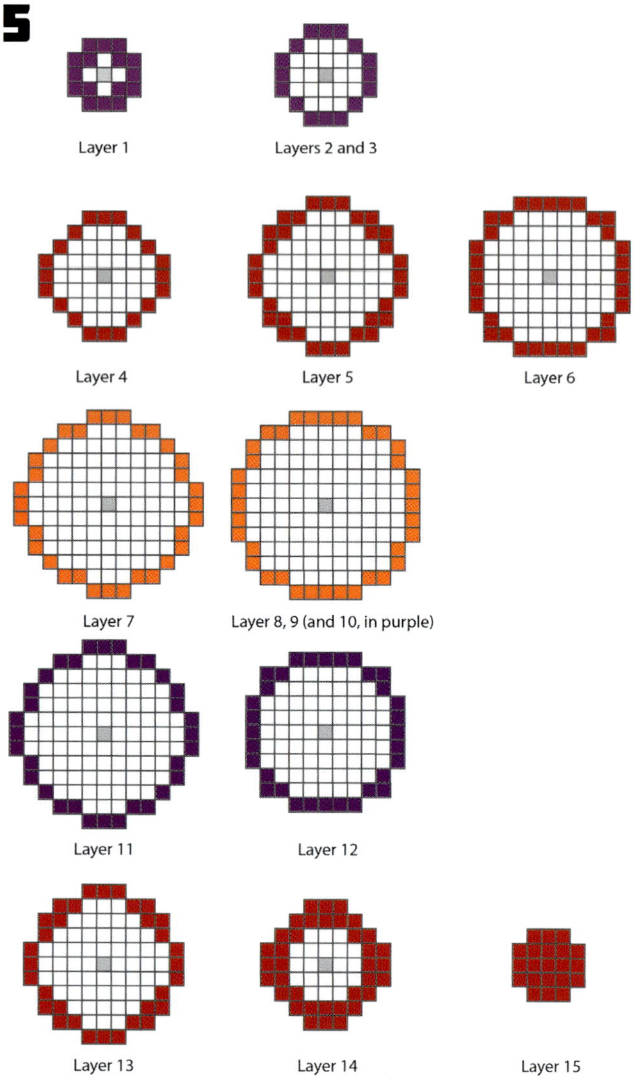

The rest of the build is placing circles of wool on top of each other. The balloon diagram shows where each block of wool is placed at each layer. Follow the patterns carefully to make sure the center of each circle is the same as the circle below. You can run a column of temporary blocks like dirt up from the center of the basket to help with this. The white squares are empty spaces. The gray square shows the center but is also empty.

Layers 1, 2, and 3 are purple wool. Layers 2 and 3 are the same circle.

Layers 4, 5, and 6 are red wool.

Layers 7, 8, and 9 are orange wool. Layers 8 and 9 are the same circle.

Layer 10 is purple wool, but it is the same circle as 8 and 9. Layers 11 and 12 are purple wool.

Layers 13, 14, and 15 are red wool.

CIRCLE WORK

In placing these circles, it can help to count the number of empty blocks from the center and how long the sides of the circle are. If it gets confusing to keep track, you also can try building the entire balloon in one color of wool or use a different color wool for each layer. When you are finished building the shape, you can replace wool with different colors to make stripes or other patterns.

3. ZIGGURAT

Ziggurats were massive temples built in ancient Mesopotamia.

They were built with several terraces, each smaller than the one below, and flat roofs. Here's a smaller-sized one that would still make a fairly large base! This ziggurat is based on the Great Ziggurat of Ur, which has three front staircases.

MATERIALS

78½ stacks smooth sandstone
10 stacks grass blocks
48 sandstone stairs
63 sandstone slabs
12 spruce wood doors
105 dark oak wood fences

Build the foundation of the ziggurat out of smooth sandstone using the diagram. The wall is 2 blocks thick with indentations, and the inside space of this foundation is 29 blocks by 29 blocks. Notice that at the center of the side and back walls there is a 3-block indent. The other indents are 2 blocks wide. Build this shape up to be 7 blocks high.

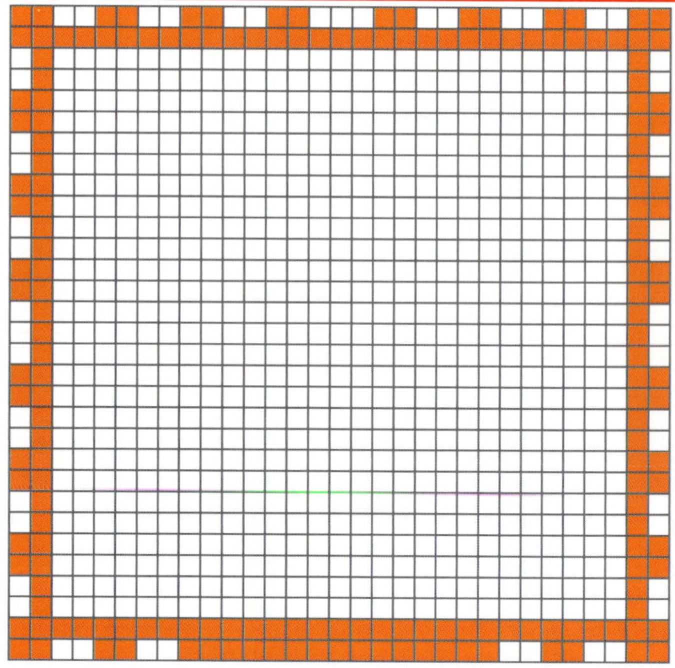

Ground floor

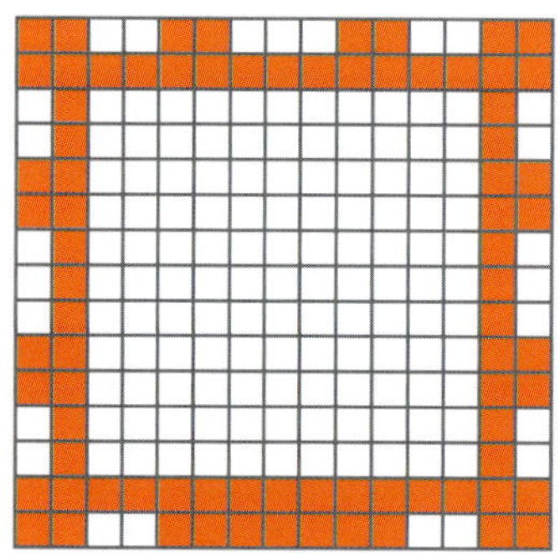

Second floor

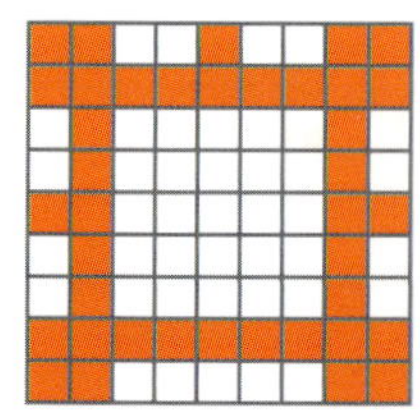

Third floor

On the outer faces of the walls, build another wall 2 blocks high and 1 block thick.

Add grass along the inside of the walls, 1 block down from the wall placed in step 2. The grass should be 7 blocks wide on all sides. Fill the empty square inside the grass sides with sandstone. This is the base of the second floor.

Use the diagram to create the bottom layer of the second floor's walls. Like the ground floor's walls, it is 2 blocks thick with indentations.

Build this wall up to be 6 blocks high.

On the outer faces of the wall, build another wall that is 2 blocks high and 1 block thick.

Add a smooth sandstone floor 1 block down from the top of these walls.

8

In the center of this floor, add the bottom layer for a third floor using the diagram.

9

Build these walls up to be 5 blocks high.

10

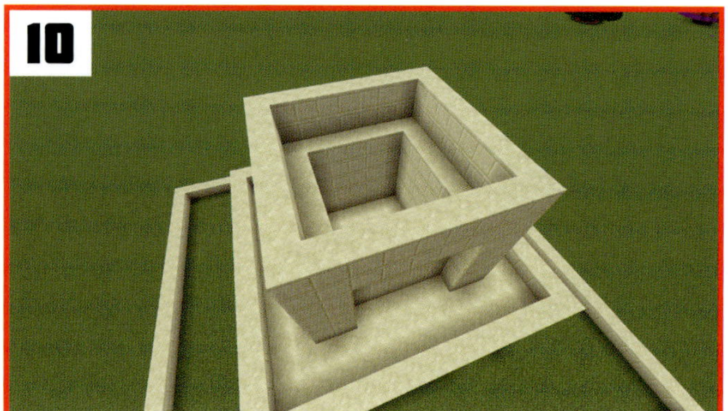

On the outer faces of these walls, build another wall 2 blocks high and 1 block thick.

11

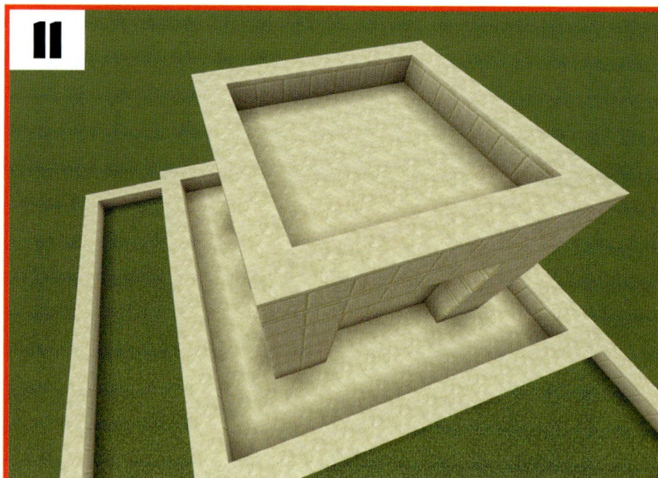

One block down from the top of these walls, add a sandstone floor.

12

On this last floor, add a 5x5 square that is 4 blocks high.

13

Fill in this top floor with sandstone.

14

The structure of the main building is done, so it is ready for details. At each of the top corners of the outer walls, place 2 blocks of sandstone on top of each other. Place a sandstone block on either side of this pillar. Do this at each of the four levels.

15

On the top level, add dark oak fences between the corners.

16

On the third floor, break an opening that is 3 blocks high and 3 blocks wide. Break an additional block at the top to make an arch.

17

Add dark oak fences to the sides and top of this arch.

18

On the front of the second floor, add two sets of double spruce doors in the indents.

In the center of the ground floor, break a 3x3-block opening.

Add two upside-down stairs on either side of the opening to create an arch.

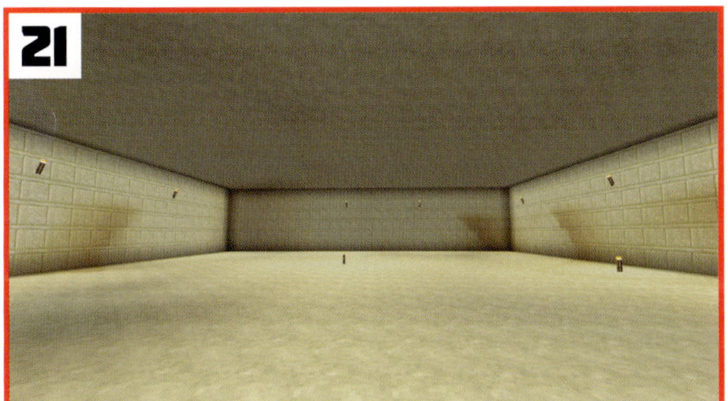

Inside the ground floor, add a ceiling of sandstone to cover the grass blocks. Then replace the grass blocks with sandstone to finish the floor.

On the second floor, add blocks for the base of a staircase to the third floor. These stepped blocks are 3 blocks wide and, at the bottom, 4 deep.

23

Add 5 rows of sandstone stairs to these stepped blocks, up to the wall.

24

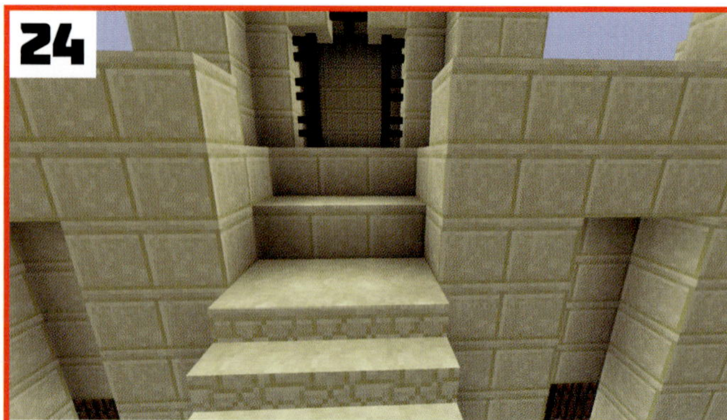

Break 4 blocks in the outer wall and 2 blocks of the inner wall to make space for more stairs.

25

Add 2 more rows of stairs to reach the third floor.

26

Add sandstone blocks to both sides of the staircase as railings.

27

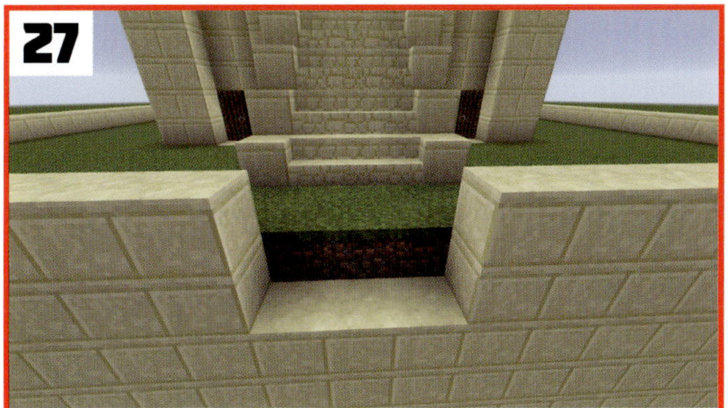

Now add the stairs from the bottom floor to the second floor. First, break a 3-block gap in the wall at the front of the second floor.

28

Add a 5x5 platform 1 block below the grass.

29

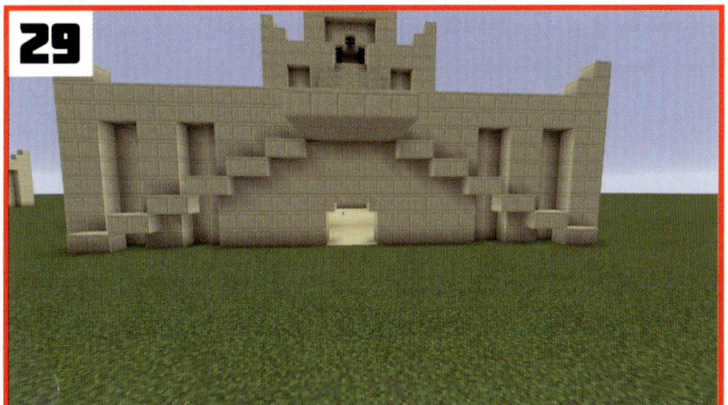

On one side of this platform, build 6 stepped rows of 2 sandstone blocks each to the ground. Do this on the other side of the platform as well.

30

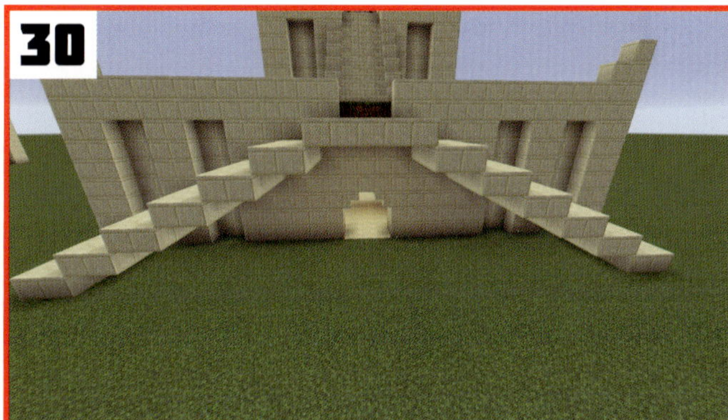

Extend these steps to be 5 blocks wide.

31

Create an identical set of 6 stepped rows in the front of the platform. They are 5 blocks wide, with each step 2 blocks deep.

32

Add 7 rows of 3 sandstone slabs to each of these 3-block staircases to create slab staircases. Each row is centered on the steps, as shown.

33

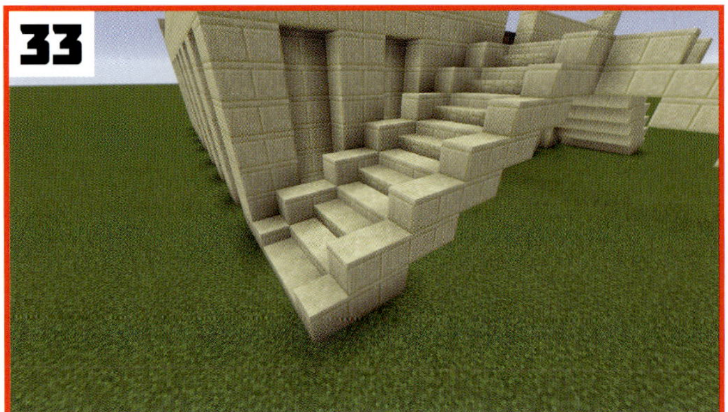

Add blocks on top of the outer sides of the 3 staircases as railings.

34

Build the outer railings of each staircase down to the ground to be walls.

35

Add two walls that are 5 blocks long in each of the two corners made by the staircases.

36

Build these up to be 5 blocks high to create the front buildings of the ziggurat. Fill the top of these buildings with grass.

37

At each outer corner of these two platforms, add a 2-block pillar of sandstone with a block of sandstone on either side, as in step 16.

38

On each outside wall of the front buildings, add 3 columns of sandstone 4 blocks tall, spaced 1 block apart. Add sandstone stairs at the top of each column.

Between each column, 3 blocks up, add an upside-down stair.

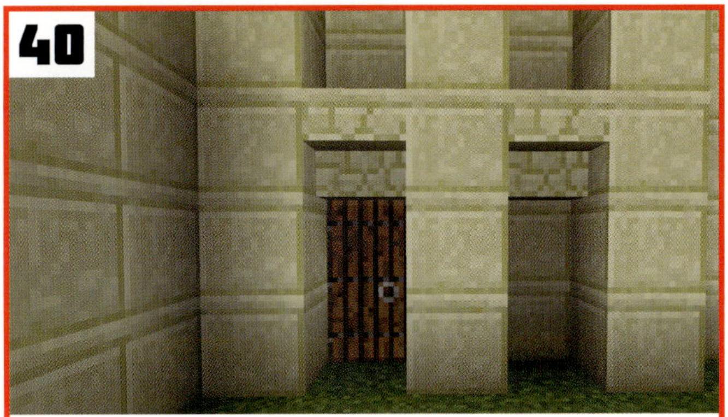

On the sides of each of the front buildings, add 1 spruce door.

Inside each front room, break open an entrance to the interior of the ziggurat steps.

On the 5x5 platform below the second floor, add a 4-block column of sandstone to each corner.

Add a 5x5 sandstone roof above the columns.

At each corner of the roof, add a 2-block column of sandstone. On each side of these columns, add a block of sandstone.

45

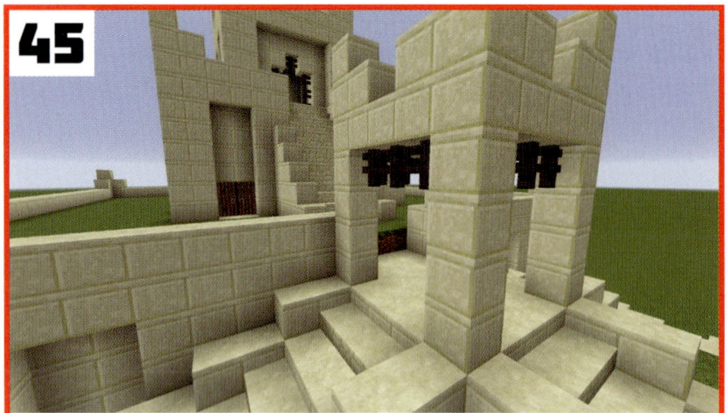

Add 3 dark oak fences between each column of this platform.

46

Add 3 sandstone stairs to reach the grass of the second level.

47

Add dark oak fences at the top of each indentation in the main building's walls.

Add floors and rooms to the interior of the ziggurat as you like and plants to the grassy areas. I've added jungle leaf blocks and jungle trees. You may also want to add some windows, even though they aren't a traditional part of ziggurats, or try patterned terracotta in the wall indents. Move in and enjoy the splendor.

SCAFFOLDING

Usually you will need some scaffolding to stand on as you build. These are just temporary blocks that you will remove once your build is done or when you no longer need them. One of the best scaffolding blocks is dirt. You won't mistake it for the real build (unless you are building a dirt house!), plus it is easy to break.

4. HEDGE MAZE

Humans have built mazes, puzzling collections of paths of wrong and right turns, for thousands of years.

The oldest known mazes were built in Egypt and Crete four thousand years ago. Some of the most beautiful mazes today are hedge mazes built out of shaped bushes. You can find patterns for mazes in books and online, and you can also invent your own maze puzzles. This build is based on a diagram that shows exactly where the hedge walls and passageways go. If you'd like to design your own, there are tips for doing so at the end of this chapter.

MATERIALS

63 stacks oak leaves
42 stacks podzol (optional)*
6 stone bricks
3 mossy stone bricks
8 stone brick stairs
1 stone brick slab
Additional materials for maze center

*If you use podzol for the paths and under the hedge walls

Substitutions: You can use any type of leaves for your maze and any block you like for the paths and ground beneath the leaf blocks.

1

Before and after flattening the land. At the edges of the flat area, you can add and remove dirt blocks to make the plot look more natural.

Clear out or create a flat area that is about 57x57. This is a big area, so it will be easier to flatten out land that is already pretty flat, like in the plains or even a desert. The maze itself is 52x52, and you'll want a little space on all sides.

CLEARING GRASS

You can pour buckets of water to quickly clear grass and flowers from the ground.

2

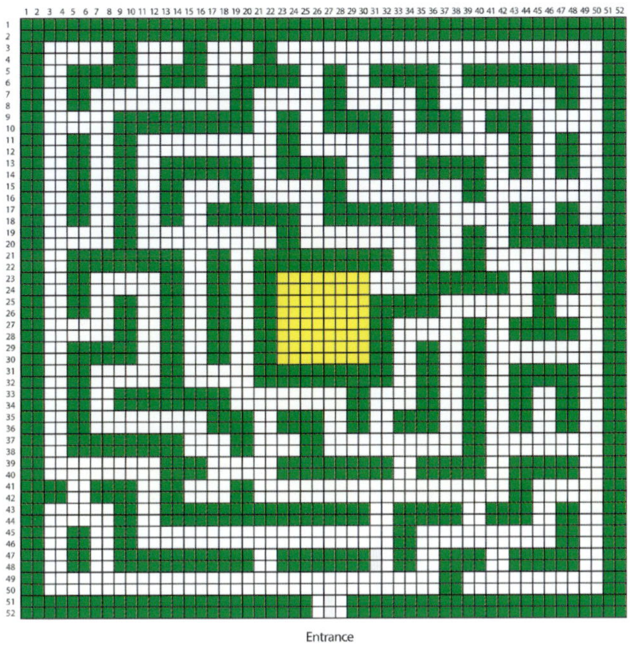

Use the maze diagram to construct the maze. You can either place your leaf blocks to create the hedge maze walls or place path blocks to create the pathways, or you can switch between both methods. I found it easier to create the pathways first and then add the maze walls. If you do pathways first, you'll want to pick a special block for your paths. I chose podzol. As you build the maze, make sure the walls and the pathways are all 2 blocks wide. The hedge walls should be 3 blocks tall. However, you can build them just 1 block tall at first. Then, when you're sure you have the walls in the right places, build them up to 3 blocks tall. This maze leaves a central area that is 15x15 blocks square. The entrance is 3 blocks wide.

COUNTING BY FIVES

To help count long distances, it can help to place a temporary block every 5 or 10 blocks. That way you can recount quickly to 5, 10, 15, etc. if you forget where you are. To do this, as you count, you leave block 1, 2, 3, and 4 empty and on block 5 place a wool block (or other temporary block).

3

At the front entryway, build 2 columns of stone brick blocks, 3 blocks high.

PLACING STAIRS

How the stairs place depends on where you put your cursor.

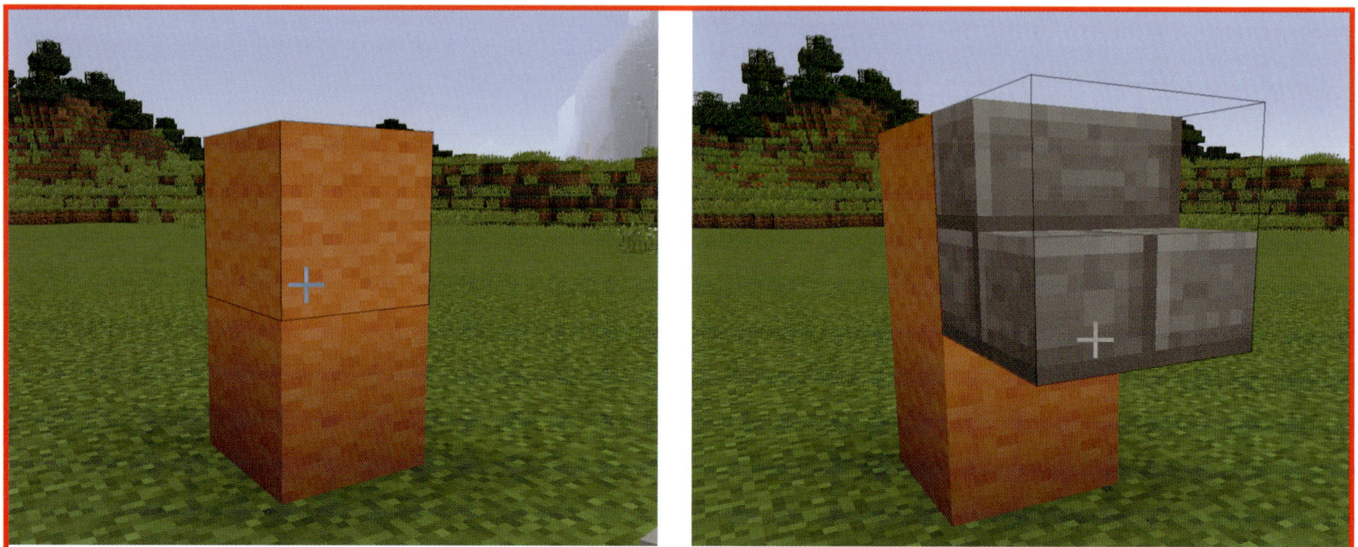

To place stairs right side up against a block, aim your cursor at the bottom of that block.

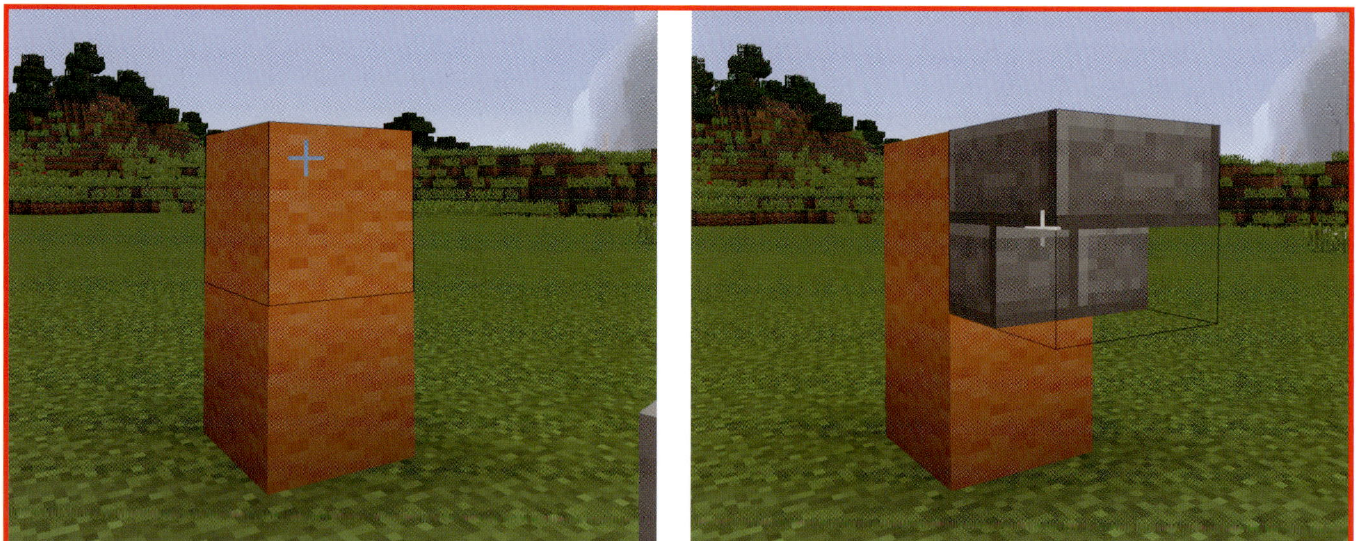

To place stairs upside down, aim your curse at the top of the block.

4

Place stone brick stair blocks on top of each column, as shown.

5

Against each stair block, place upside-down stone brick stairs.

6

Above the upside-down stairs, place a row of 3 stone bricks.

7

Above the central stone brick block, place a stone brick slab.

8

Add finishing details to the archway. Replace 4 of the stone brick blocks with mossy stone bricks for a weathered look. Add stone brick stairs on the outside and front of the stone brick columns.

Decorate the center of the maze however you want. I added a few blocks of gold and emerald and a little treasure in a chest.

DESIGNING YOUR OWN MAZE PUZZLE

To create your own puzzle for the 51x52 maze, first build 5 concentric squares of leaf blocks, 2 blocks wide, with 2-block wide paths between. This step will help keep your pathways and hedges 2 blocks apart from each other as you design the puzzle. For now, keep the hedges 1 block high. (You can also use pencil and paper to follow these steps.)

Then use temporary blocks, like yellow wool, to mark out the path that will lead to the solution. You will want to break open some existing hedge walls to travel between the concentric squares.

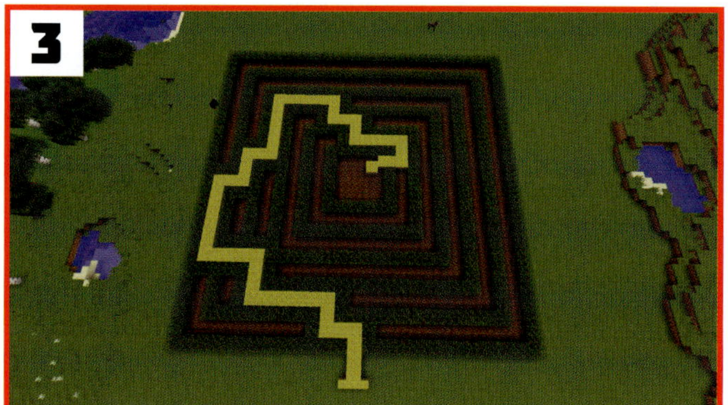

Add hedge walls to block off the yellow wool path. You may decide to undo some of these walls in the next step, but these help to make sure your solution is difficult to find.

Now use a different temporary block, like magenta wool, to mark out all of the wrong paths. Create new hedge walls to break up the original concentric paths as you go. I've also used red wool to show where the wrong paths and the right path connect. This way I can make sure I haven't accidentally created a solution that I don't want or a solution that is easier.

When you are satisfied with your puzzle, take the wool out and build the hedge walls up to be 3 blocks high.

5. WINDMILL

Windmills were used in the past to grind grains like wheat into flour or to pump water from the ground.

Their arms, called sails (or blades), rotated in a large circle when they were pushed by the wind. The arms were connected to gears inside the building. Their rotation forced the gears and machinery inside to turn as well. This action was used to grind flour or move water.

MATERIALS

4½ stacks dark oak planks
28 dark oak fences
49 stone bricks
2½ stacks brick stairs
40 white wool
17 light blue stained glass pane
3 spruce logs
1 spruce door
1 wooden trapdoor

Substitutions: Use different woods in place of the dark oak planks or cobblestone instead of stone bricks.

1

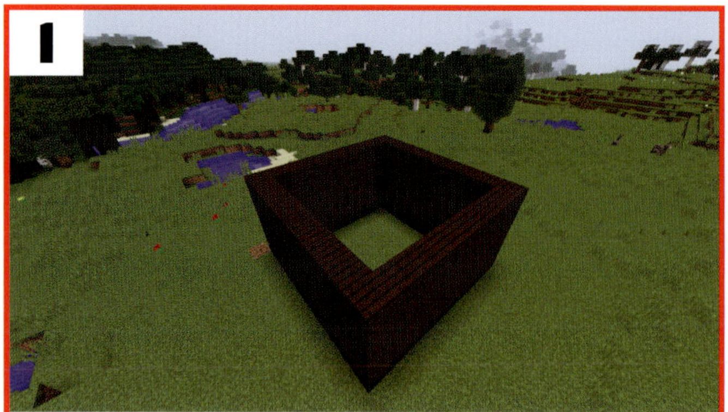

Using dark oak, build a 9x9 square 5 blocks high.

2

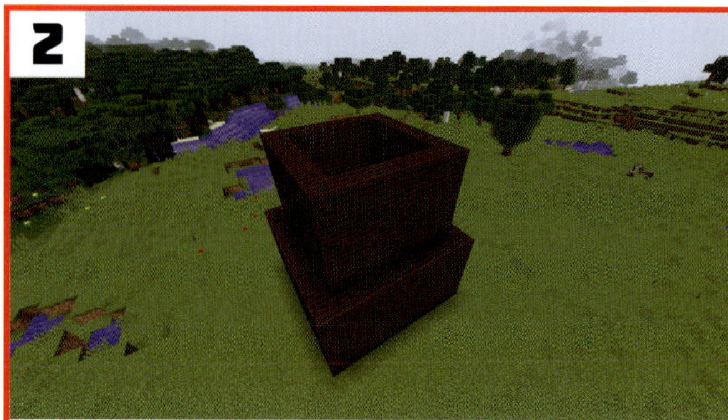

Above this, use dark oak to build a 7x7 square 4 blocks high.

3

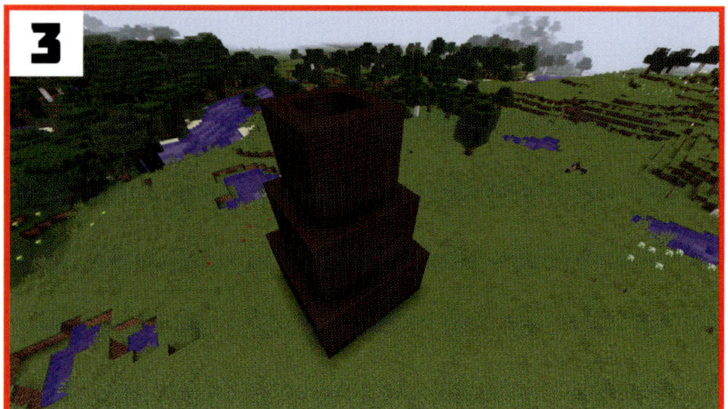

Finally, still using dark oak, build a 5x5 square 5 blocks high.

4

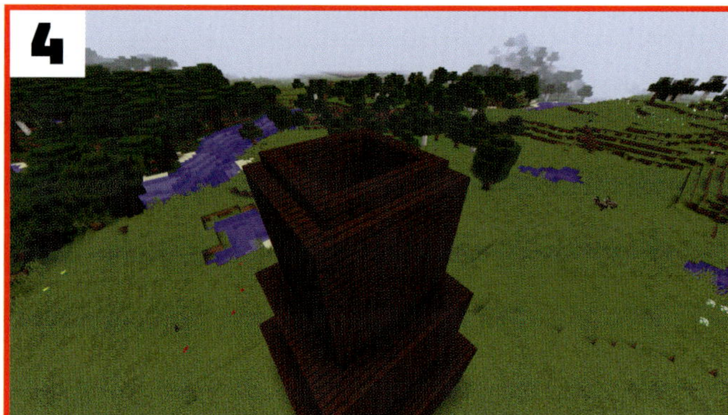

On top of the 5x5 walls, place dark oak stairs. Fill in this level with dark oak planks.

5

One block below the oak stairs, place stone brick stairs all around the walls.

6

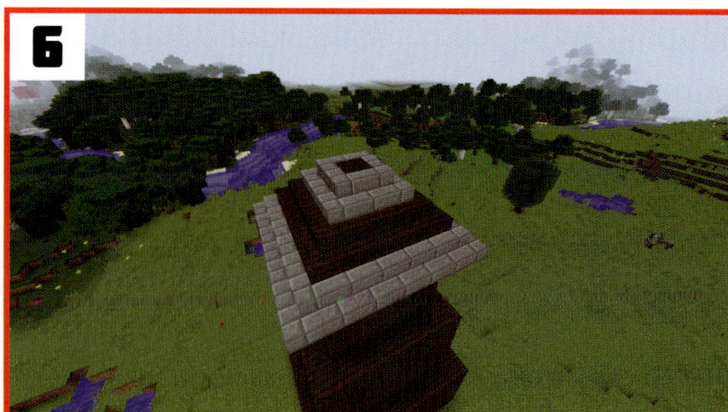

In the center of the top platform, place a single block of dark oak planks and surround this block with stone brick stairs.

7

Top the single dark oak planks block with 2 blocks of stone brick.

8

Now that the main structure is done, let's add details. At each corner of each wall, replace the dark oak with a column of stone bricks.

9

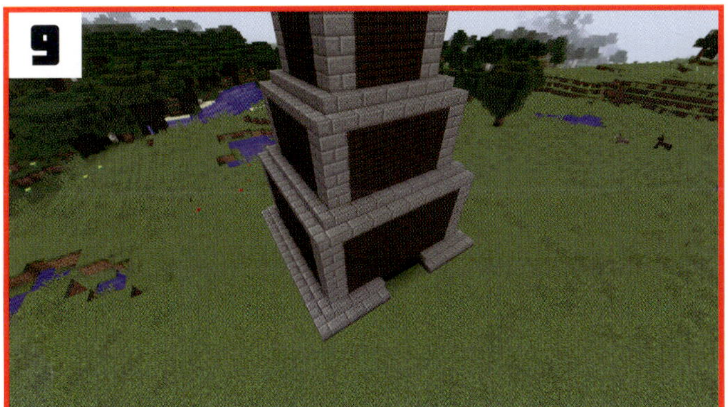

Surround the base of each of the three rooms with stone brick stairs. Leave a 3-block gap in the center of the bottom room.

10

Place a spruce door in the center of this gap. Replace the dark oak on its sides and top with stone brick as a frame.

11

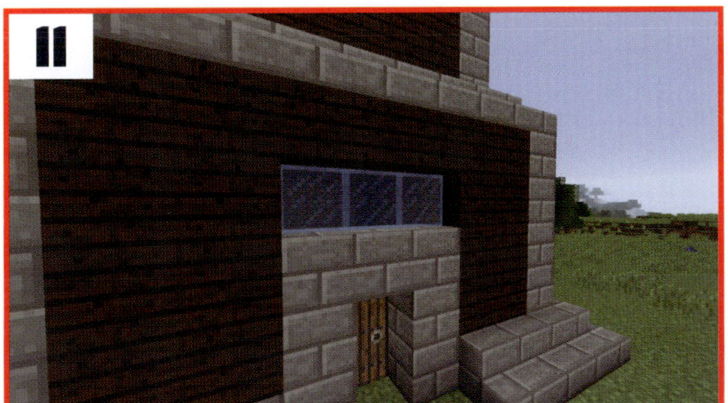

Above the top frame of the door, place a row of 3 light blue stained glass panes.

12

Above the glass panes, place 3 upside-down stone brick stairs.

13

In the center of each of the 3 other sides of the bottom floor, add a window of 2 light-blue stained glass panes. Above the glass, place an upside-down stone brick stair, and below it place a regular stone brick stair.

14

Create similar windows on each side of the top 2 floors—except here the windows are only 1 glass pane high.

15

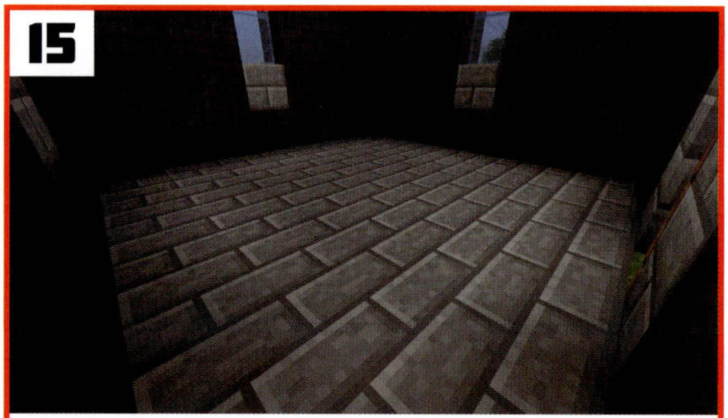

Inside the windmill, use stone bricks as the floor. If you like, use stone bricks to create additional floors at the second and third levels. In a small building like this, it is more space-efficient to use ladders to reach the upper floors than to use stairs.

16

Now it is time to make the sails (or blades) of the windmill. First, replace the stone brick stairs right below the front top window of the windmill with a full block of stone brick.

Place 3 spruce logs extending out from this stone brick block. On the last log, place a wooden trapdoor.

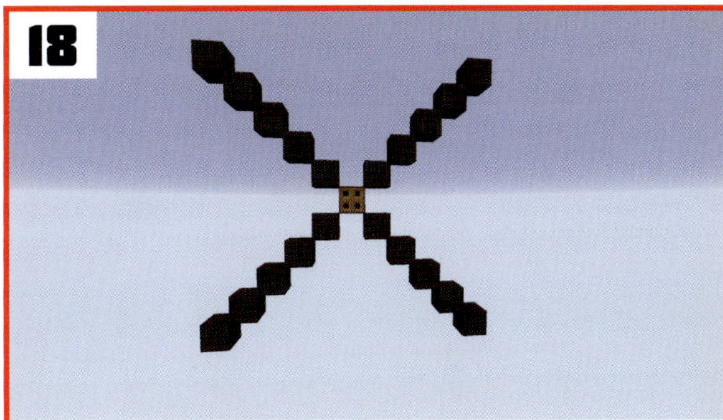

Build the base of each sail out from the last spruce log diagonally. Use 5 dark oak planks for each arm.

For the top right sail, place 2 white wool blocks on top of each of the 5 dark oak planks. I'll call each of these 2-block stacks a column of white wool, for a total of 5 columns.

On top of the first 3 columns of white wool, place 2 dark oak fences. On the fourth column of white wool, place 1 dark oak fence.

21

For the top left sail, repeat this pattern, but place the white wool blocks and the fencing to the left of each of the 5 dark oak planks.

22

For the bottom left sail, place the white wool blocks and fencing beneath the dark oak planks.

23

For the bottom right sail, place the wool and fences to the right of the dark oak planks.

And that's it! Your windmill is done, and now you can decorate the inside and outside as you like.

6. PUMPKIN HOUSE

Building giant 3D versions of real-life objects is pretty fun, especially if you build them large enough to live in. Once you have found pumpkins in the wild to make seeds and grow more pumpkins, this house made of pumpkins is very economical, too!

Before you start, remember that Minecraft pumpkins have to be placed on a surface, so you will need plenty of temporary blocks, like dirt, to place the pumpkins on as you construct each layer. Because of this factor and because it can be hard to build circles on top of each other, you might want to fill the interior of each pumpkin circle layer with dirt as you go. You can remove the dirt once you are finished. Also, a pumpkin will always face toward you as you place it. You may want to place all pumpkins facing inside or outside the house, or facing all to the back or front or sides. If you don't like the faces, you can point them all to the inside of the house and then cover the inside walls with another block you like.

MATERIALS

8½ stacks pumpkins
10 lime-green wool
23 green wool
1 dark oak door
18 orange stained glass blocks
Additional blocks for interior floor

Substitutions: A different orange block, like orange wool or orange concrete, will work well in place of the pumpkins. Green concrete will work for the stem and leaves.

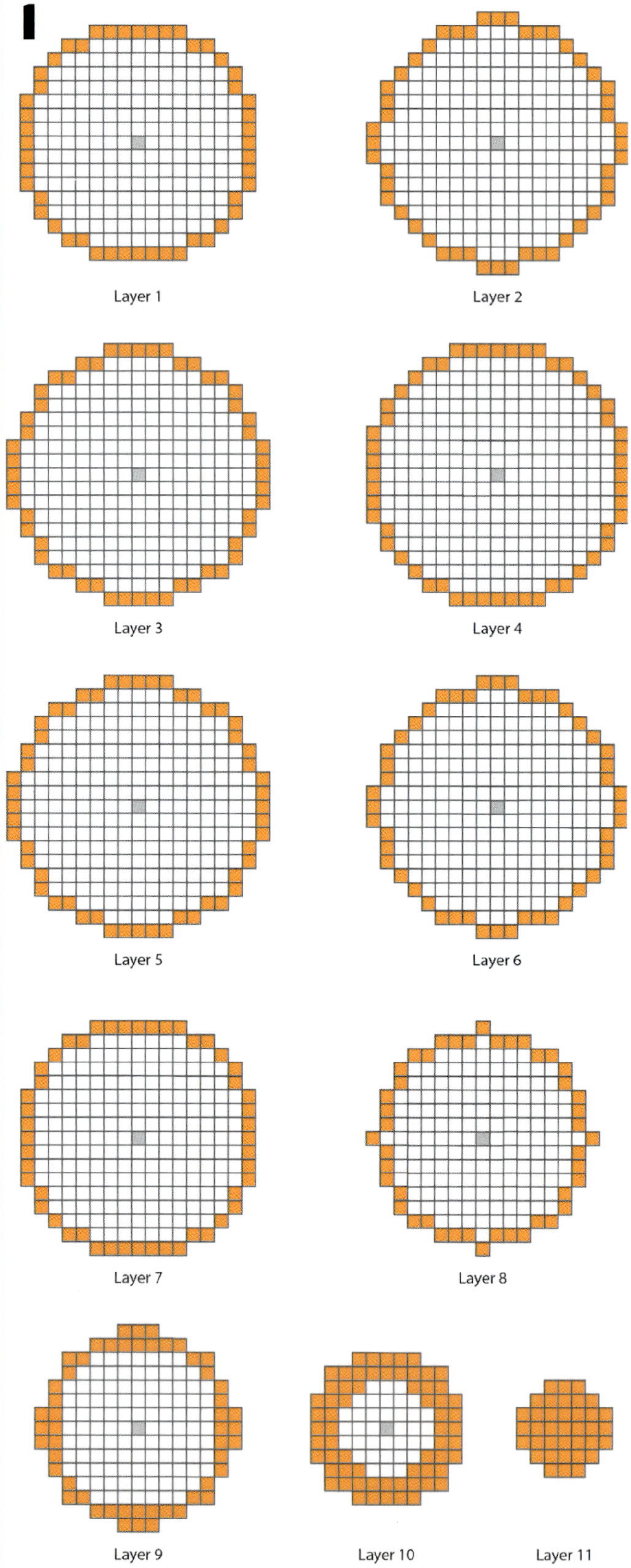

Because the pumpkin house is a flattened sphere, each layer of blocks is different from the layer beneath it. Start with level 1 as the bottom layer and place the pumpkins as the grid shows you for that level. The grid shows block by block the orange squares, which should be pumpkins, and the white squares, which should be empty. The gray square is the center (empty), shown to help with counting.

2

Once you've finished your pumpkin, add the stem. Place a cross shape of green wool on the center of the roof. Then add an identical second layer.

3

To curve the stalk to the left, we will stack 3 more cross shapes of green wool on top of each other, but with each cross 1 block to the left of the cross below it. The middle of the first of these crosses should be on top of the leftmost block of the stalk. These images show the crosses as lime green to help distinguish them. However, build these yourself using regular green wool.

Now add a leaf on the other side of the stalk. First, place 4 blocks of lime-green wool diagonally and to the right of the second layer of the stalk, as shown.

On either side of the middle 2 lime-green wool blocks, place another lime-green block of wool.

Now the pumpkin needs a door, windows, and a floor inside to make it into a house. First, add a dark oak wood door in the center of the pumpkin's front and a 3-block wide window of orange glass above it, as shown.

In the center of the other three sides, make a cross-shaped window of orange glass.

8

Inside, you can make the floor with any blocks you like, of course. I've made circles of dark oak wood and lime-green wool that follow the shape of the pumpkin. The first circle is 1 block wide, and the next two are 2 blocks wide. I've filled the center with lime-green wool.

9

Your house is complete now! You can landscape outside and decorate inside. Outside, I've used oak leaf blocks and pumpkins to make it look like my pumpkin house is a massive pumpkin in a pumpkin patch. Torches are on top of single dark oak fences for light. Last, I've added a path down the hill made of dark oak planks, spruce logs, and dark oak stairs.

REMEMBERING CIRCLE PATTERNS

As you make more and more circles in Minecraft, you will notice that each quarter of a circle repeats the pattern in the other quarters. One way that can help with following a particular circle's shape is to remember the number of blocks in each small section of one quarter. Start with one long side and end with the last block before the next long side. For example, the circle in level 1 has sides that are 7 blocks long, which are followed by 2 blocks, then 1 block, then 2 more blocks. It's easy to remember 7, 2, 1, 2. Also, the sections next to a long side follow the same direction (horizontal or vertical) as that long side.

7. MARKET STALLS

Market stalls are a great way to share or trade goods with other players or to add a little life to a village.

You could put villagers whose trades you like in stalls (making sure to keep them safe from zombies, of course!). This build uses just two colors of wool for the stalls, but you can substitute any colors you like or use just one color at a time.

MATERIALS

28 red wool
21 white wool
3 oak wood stairs
10 oak wood fences
2 oak wood fence gates
3 chests
4 signs

Substitutions: Use different colors of wool in place of the red wool. You also can swap wood types.

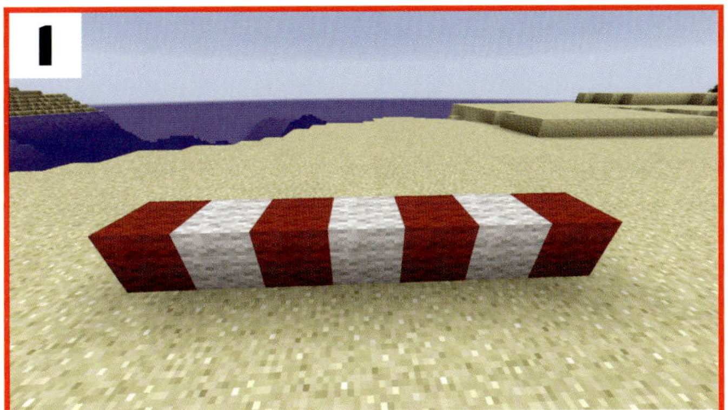

Place a row of 4 red wool blocks and 3 white wool blocks, alternating colors. This is the back wall of the market stall.

Above this row, place 2 more identical rows.

To start the roof, add a fourth row with the same pattern that is diagonal to the top row of the wall.

In front of the first roof row, place 2 more identical rows of wool.

Diagonally down and in front of to the previous row, place 1 last row of wool in the same alternating pattern.

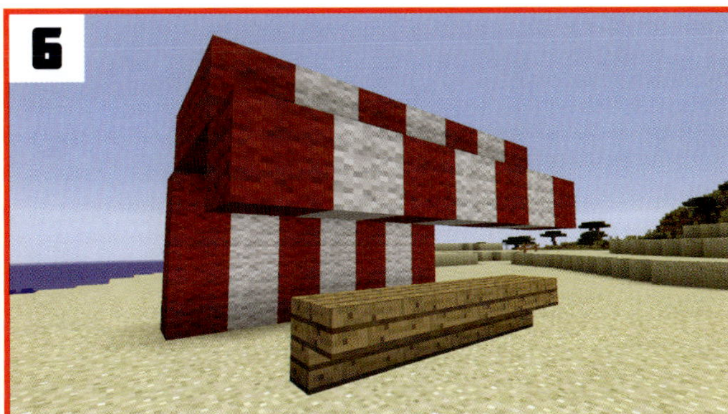

Below and centered beneath the last row of wool, place 5 upside-down oak stairs as the stall's counter.

7

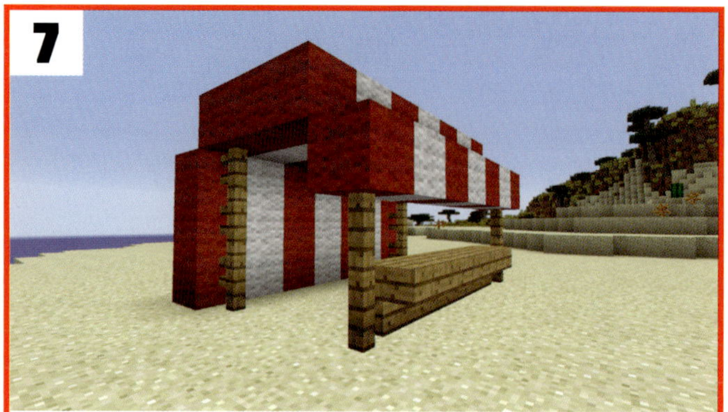

At each inside corner of the stall, place oak wood fences from the ground to the roof.

8

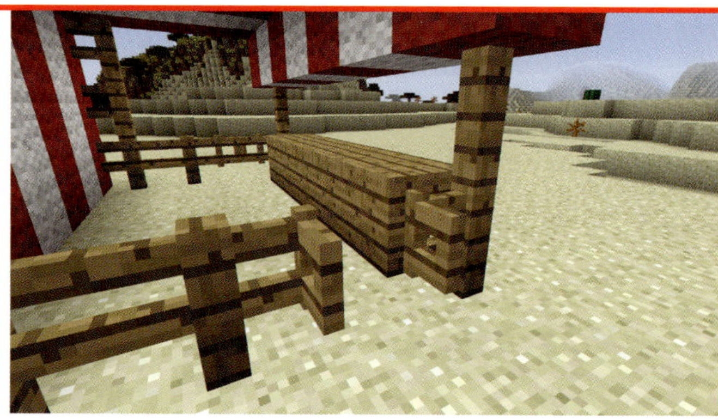

Add an extra fence and a fence gate to each side of the stall.

9

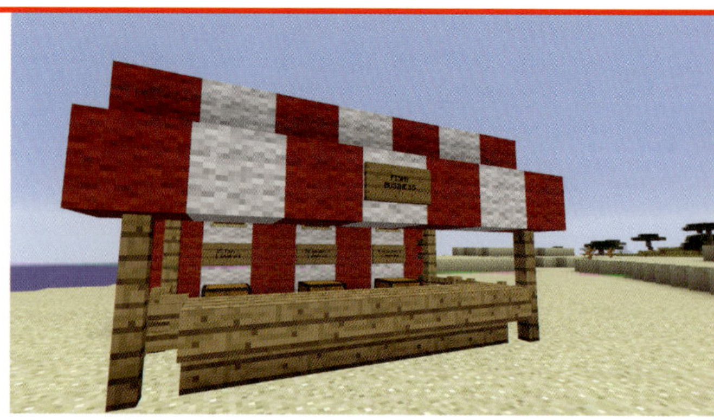

Against the back wall of the stall, place chests for goods and signs to announce prices. You can also use item frames to hold examples of the wares. Use signs on the front of the stall for your stall's name.

8. GIANT WATER SLIDE

One of the most unique elements of Minecraft is being able to move and place items freely.

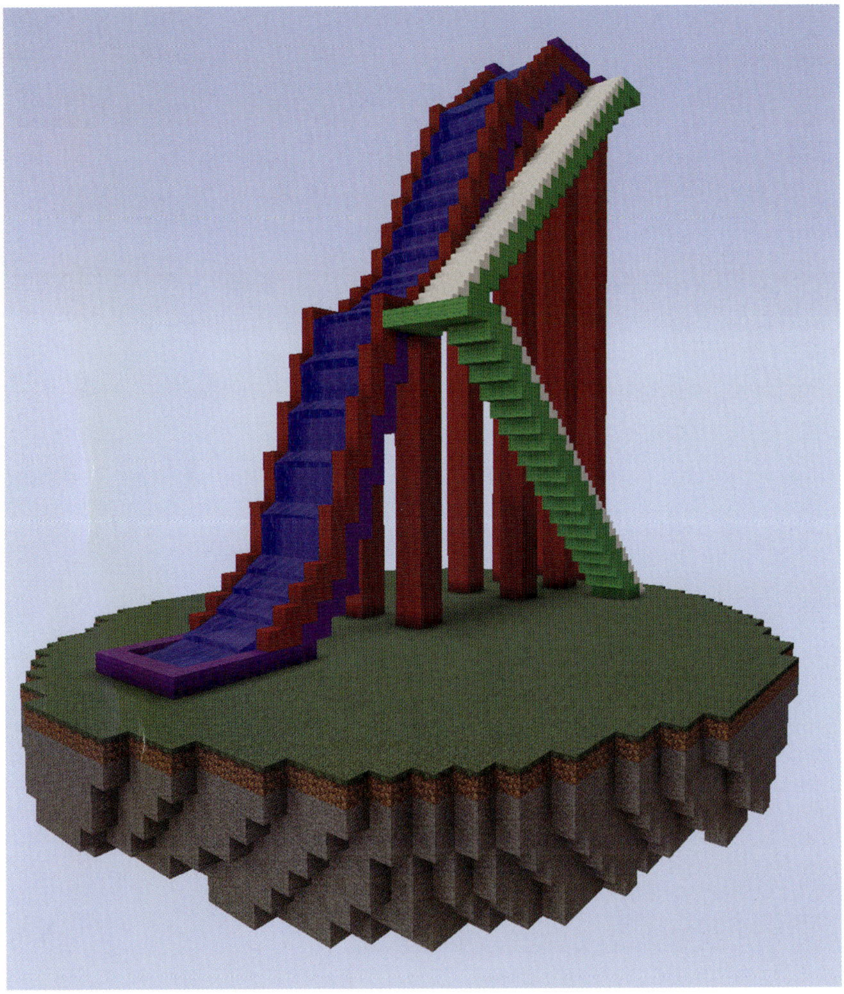

You can even place water, which will flow and move items in its way. It can move mobs, items, and you, too. And going down a massive water slide can feel real enough to give you that funny roller coaster lurch in your tummy.

MATERIALS

20 stacks red wool
9 stacks purple wool
4½ stacks lime-green wool
2 stacks quartz stairs
Buckets of water

Substitutions: Use any brightly colored wool, terracotta, or concrete.

Use purple wool to make a 5x4 rectangle level with the ground.

Add a wall of purple wool that is 1 block high on top of this rectangle.

At the back of this rectangle, add 2 more rows of purple wool inside the wall to finish the end base of the slide.

4

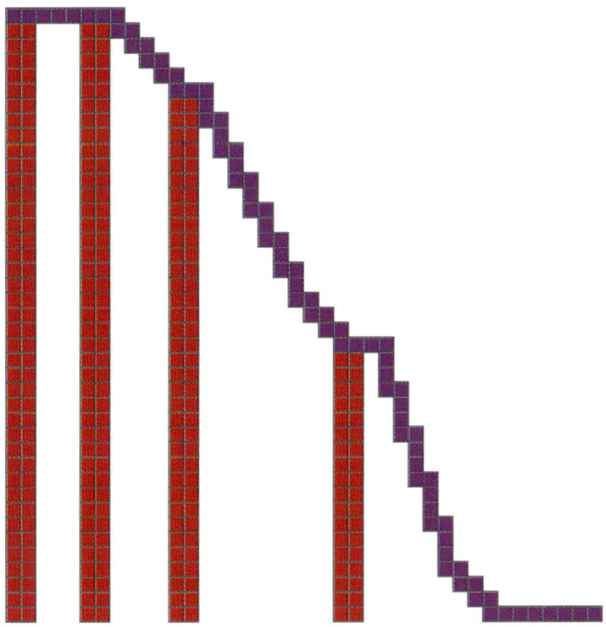

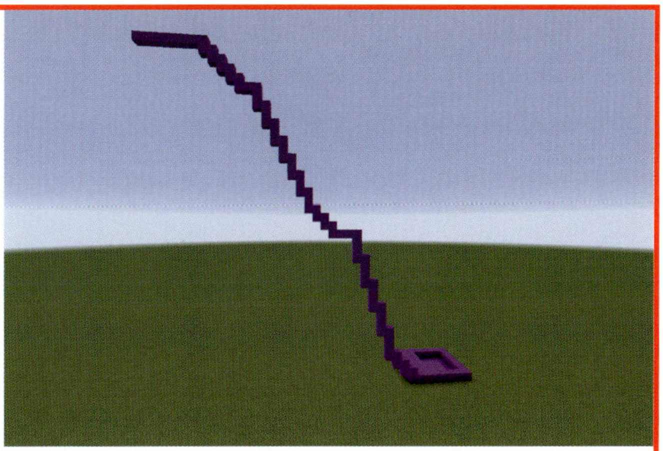

Starting with the back left side of the base, build the slope of the slide by moving up and back 1 block at a time, following the diagram.

5

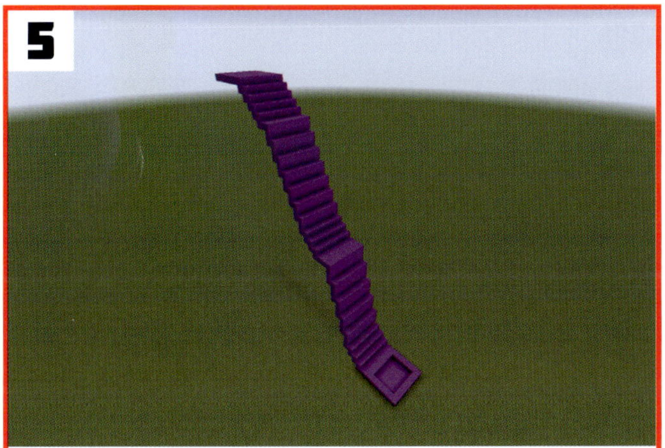

When you finish constructing the slope, build the slide out to the right to be 7 blocks wide.

6

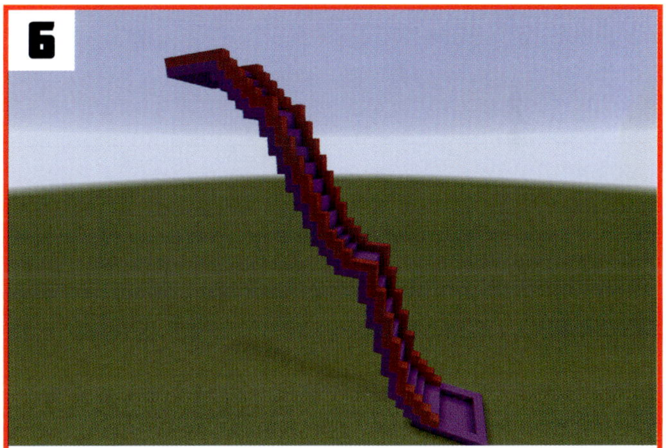

Add red-wool walls that are 1 block high above the outer edges of the slide, as shown.

7

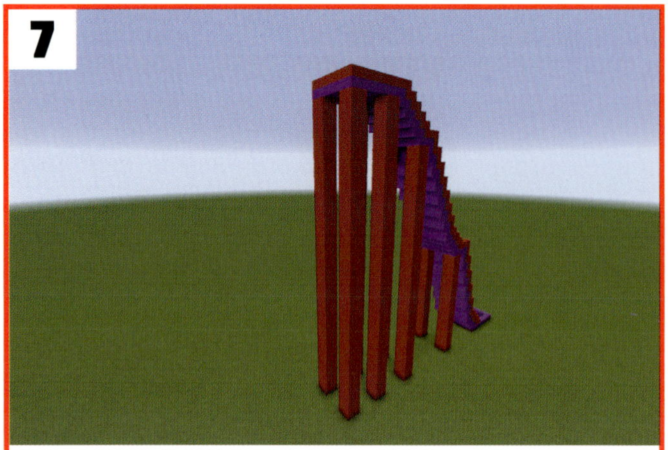

Add four pairs of 2x2 square pillars (8 pillars total) of red wool from the slide to the ground. Use the diagram to help locate where these supporting columns go.

8

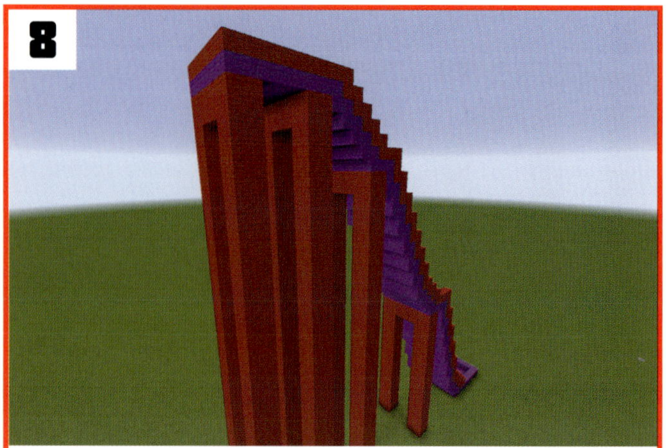

Between each pair of columns, right beneath the slide, add a horizontal beam, 2x2 square, of red wool blocks.

9

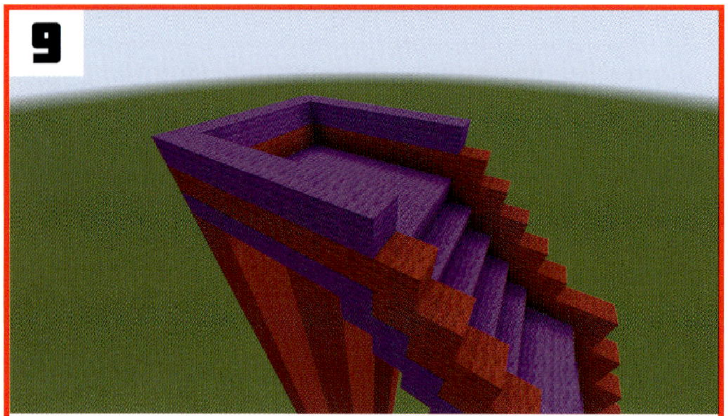

At the top of the slide, add a row of purple wool above the red walls, as shown.

10

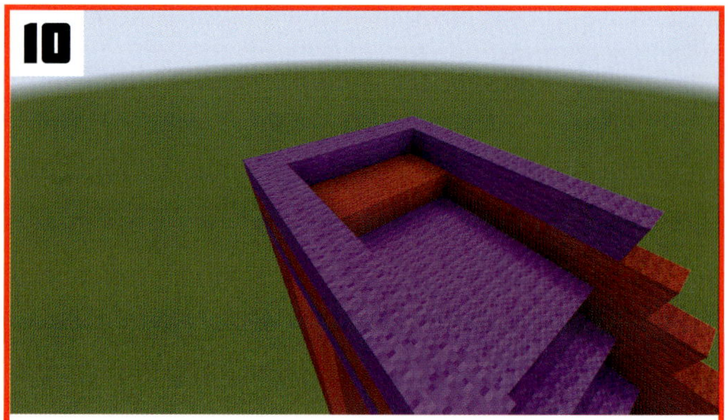

At the back of the launching area, add 2 rows of red wool.

11

Now we'll add stairs to reach the top platform. On the right side of the slide, break 2 purple wool blocks in the top wall, as shown.

12

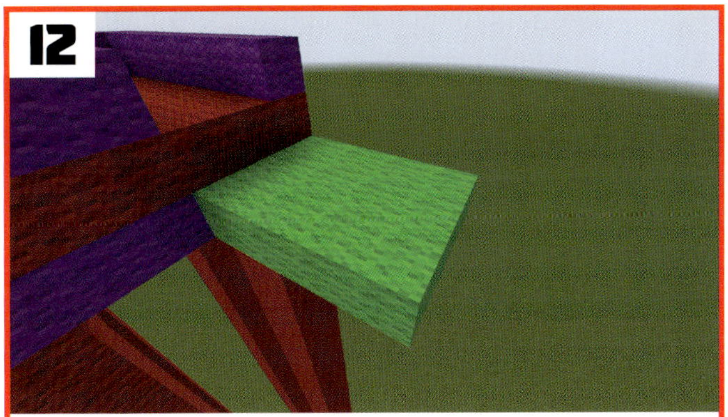

One block below this, add a 2x3 platform of lime-green wool blocks.

13

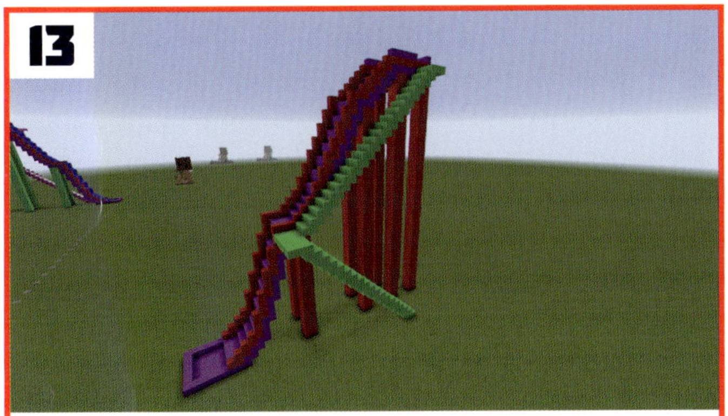

Use lime-green wool to build the base for the stairs. Build down 3 blocks wide, dropping 1 block at a time. Half way down, create a 3x6 platform. From there build the stairs in the opposite direction, toward the back of the slide.

14

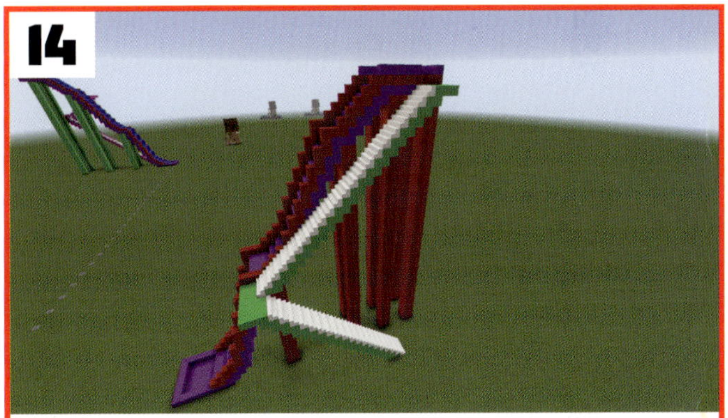

Add quartz stairs above the lime-green wool to complete the stairs.

15

Now just add water! Place 5 buckets of water at the top of the slide, against the red wool at the back. Jump in and enjoy the ride. (To move faster down the slide, press W as you go!)

9. ROCKET SHIP

This classic sci-fi rocket ship is really easy to build, and it looks amazing in a Mesa Biome.

You also could build a launching platform for it with scaffolding supports around it. Now all we need are some Minecraft planets to visit!

MATERIALS

6 stacks iron blocks
94 red terracotta
16 cyan terracotta
5 dispensers
4 spruce wood planks
10 ladders
6 blue stained glass blocks

Substitutions: If you don't have 373 iron blocks to spare, use white concrete. You also can use red concrete in place of the red terracotta.

Five blocks above the ground, build the first level of iron blocks as shown in the diagram. The sides of the circle are 5 blocks long, with empty spaces as the corners. There should be 4 blocks of empty space below this base of the rocket ship.

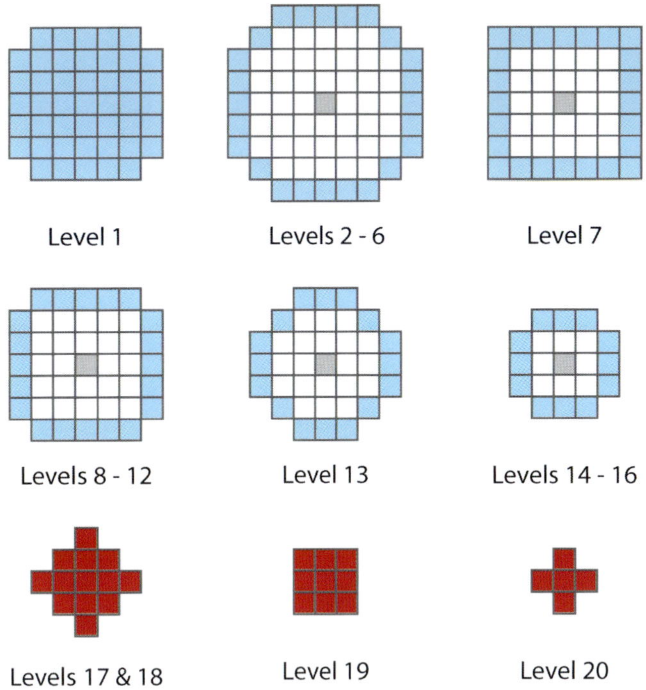

Follow the diagram to place iron block circles for levels 2 through 16 and red terracotta circles for levels 17 through 20.

Place a column of 2 blocks of red terracotta above the center of level 20.

4

Beneath the rocket ship, place a circle of cyan terracotta in the same shape as level 17.

5

Below this cyan terracotta layer, place 5 dispensers, facing down, in the same shape as level 20.

6

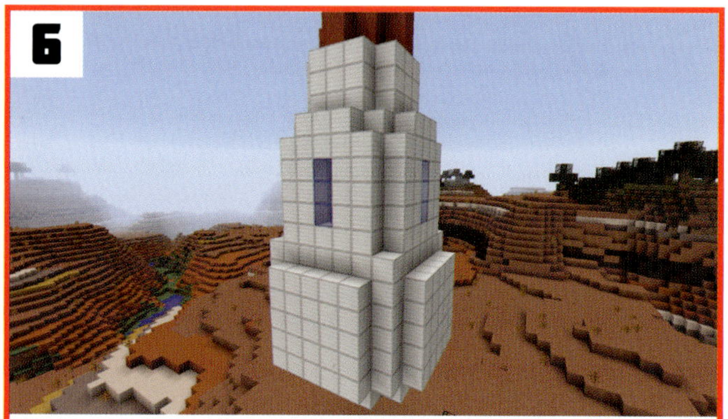

In the center of each side of the rocket's middle level, place a blue glass window that is 3 blocks high.

7

On the rocket's lower level, place a single blue glass window on each side. It should be centered and placed 1 block down from the top of this level.

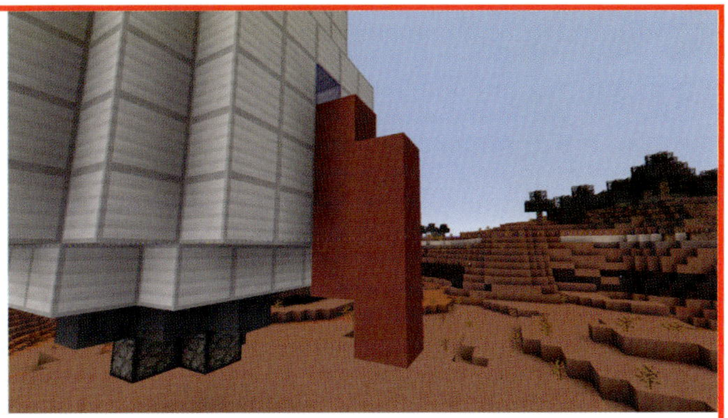

In the center of each side of the rocket's lower level, build the rocket's fins of red terracotta. First, place a 4-block column of red terracotta just below the blue window. Add another column of 4 red terracotta on the outside of the first column, but 1 block down. Finally, add another column of 6 red terracotta on the outside of the second column, but 1 block down.

Repeat step 8 on the other three sides of the rocket.

10

Now to get in the rocket! Break an outer corner of the bottom level of iron. Add a column of spruce wood planks below this to reach the ground. Place ladders up this column so you can get into your rocket.

11

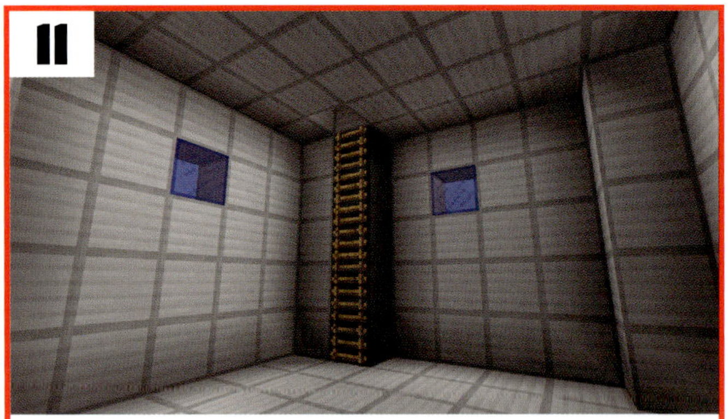

Inside, you can add a floor at the bottom of the middle level and use cyan terracotta blocks and ladders to get up there.

12

Add details as you like. You can use 2 purpur stairs as seats. Observer blocks and cyan terracotta could be the base of a control panel. You can add levers and item frames holding blocks to look like very important buttons.

10. MARS HABITAT

Build this sci-fi Mars habitat with its own enclosed greenhouse to get a little imaginary taste of living on Mars.

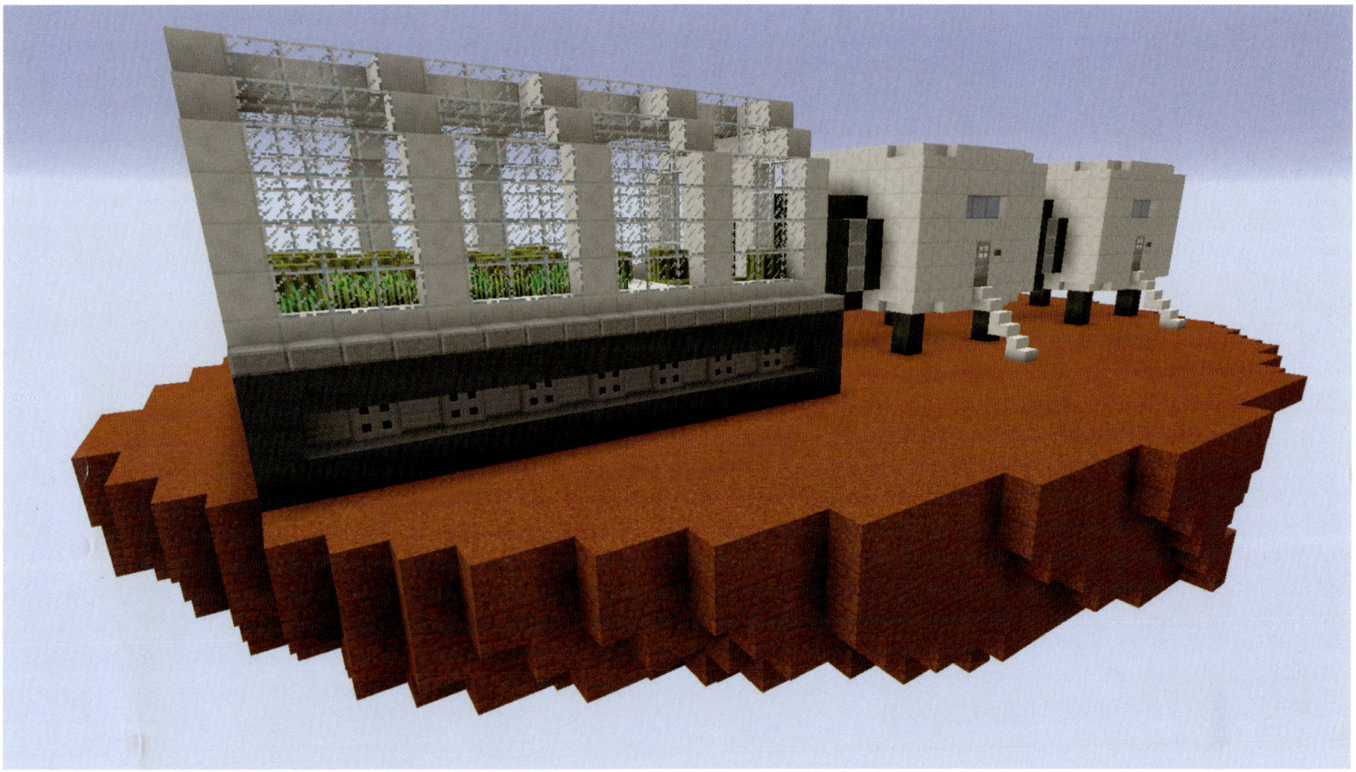

Venus is the closest planet to Earth, but it has a harsh environment that is unlikely to support any kind of life. So it is Mars, the next closest planet to Earth, that space agencies are planning to visit next, hopefully in the 2030s. The United States space agency, the National Aeronautics and Space Administration (NASA), has already sent robotic missions to Mars. You can see photographs of Mars's landscape taken by NASA's Mars rovers online at nasa.gov.

MATERIALS

12 stacks quartz blocks
63 quartz stairs
7 stacks cyan terracotta
18 light blue stained glass panes
24 white stained glass blocks
3½ stacks glass blocks
16 iron blocks
18 pistons
14 iron trapdoors
14 levers
80 dirt
2 iron doors
2 stone buttons
2 stone pressure plates
1 bucket of water

Substitutions: You can use white concrete in place of the quartz blocks, but you would still need quartz stairs to use for the white stairs. In place of pistons, you can use furnaces.

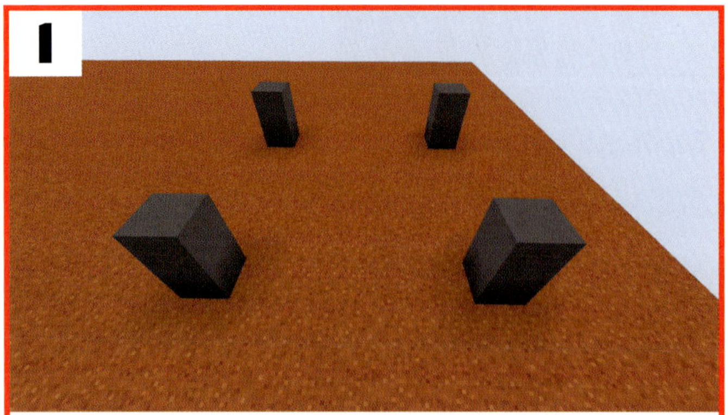

Build 4 pillars that are 2 blocks high of cyan terracotta in square. They should each be 6 blocks apart from each other (leaving 5 blocks of space between them).

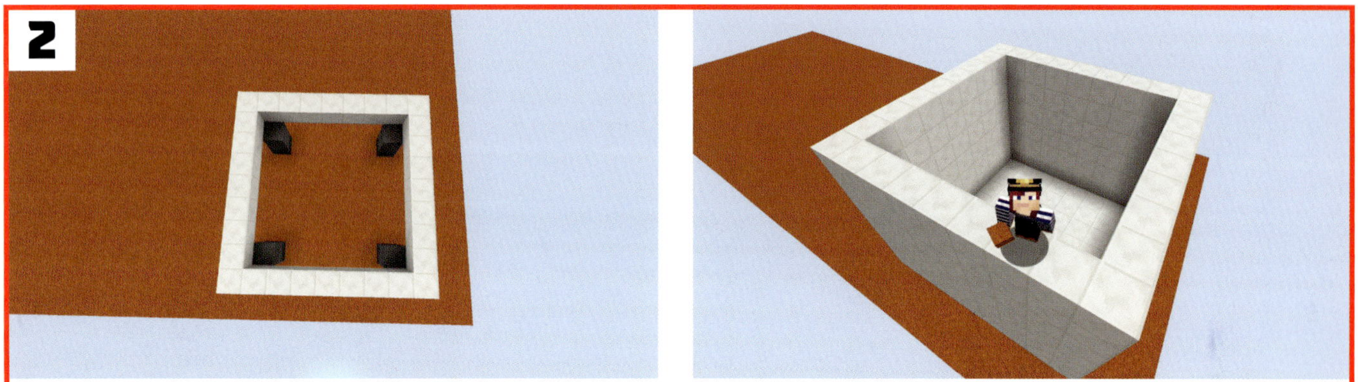

Build a 9x9 square room of quartz blocks centered on top of these posts. Build the walls 7 blocks high. The floor and ceiling should both be quartz block.

Replace the 3 outer bottom corners of the module with upside-down quartz stairs.

Replace the 3 outer top corners of the module with quartz stairs.

Add an iron door to the front of the module and a stone button to open it. (Inside the door, use a button or stone pressure plate to open the door.) Use quartz stairs to reach the door.

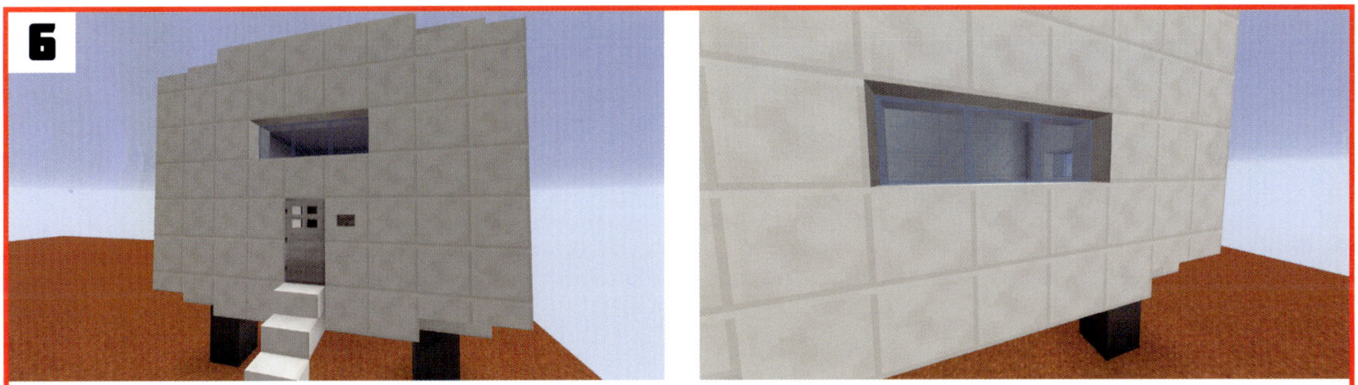

Above the door place a window that is 3 blocks long of stained light blue glass. Put the same window 1 block above the floor on the right side and back of the module.

7

Break a 3x3 hole on the left side of the module. Place 3 blocks of cyan terracotta on each side around this hole. This will be the module connector tube.

8

Build the 4 terracotta walls of the connector tube out to be 6 blocks long. On either side of the tube and 1 block from either end, add windows of white stained glass block that are 3 blocks high.

9

Build an identical module and connector tube attached to this first connector tube.

10

Now create the base of the greenhouse module. On the side of the unattached connector tube, build a 13x17 square of cyan terracotta.

11

Fill this with a filler block, like orange terracotta or oak planks.

12

One block in from the cyan terracotta, on each long side, add rows of alternating iron blocks and coal blocks.

13

On the outside of each coal block, at the top, add an iron trapdoor.

14

On the inside of each coal block, add a lever and activate it to lower the trapdoor.

15

On the two short sides of the greenhouse base, add a row of pistons facing inward. (These are decorative only, and you can use furnaces in place of them.)

16

Fill the interior of the base's second layer with a filler block.

17

Add a cyan terracotta block at each corner, outside the iron blocks and pistons. Above this, add a 13x17 rectangle of cyan terracotta identical to the first layer of the greenhouse base.

18

Add the base of the greenhouse walls using quartz block. The long walls and the wall opposite the connector tube should be 1 block in from the outer edge of the base; the wall closest to the connector tube should be flush with the base. Leave the entryway at the connector tube empty.

19

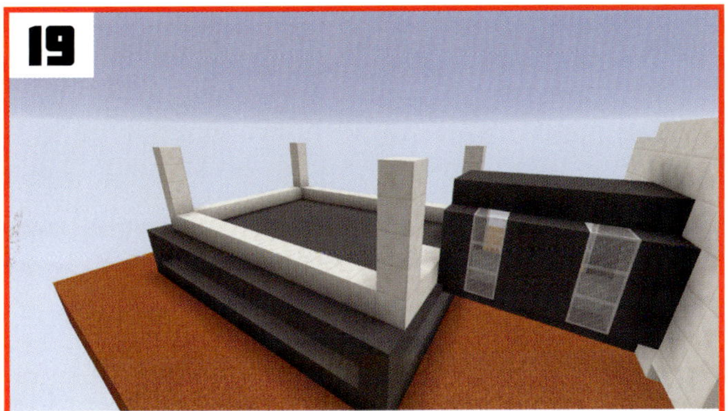

Build up the corners of the greenhouse with quartz block to be 5 blocks tall.

20

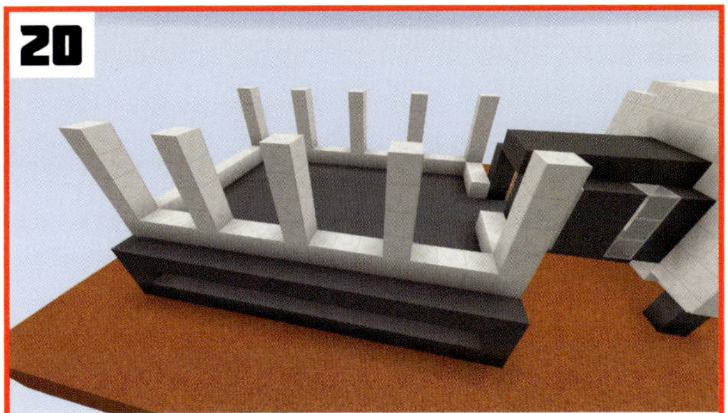

On both the long walls, add 3 more columns spaced evenly, as shown.

21

Along the wall opposite the connector tube, add 2 matching pillars in the center, as shown.

22

Above the pillars on the wall opposite the tube, place a row of quartz block 9 blocks long. Above this row, place a row of quartz 7 blocks long and centered.

On the wall of the greenhouse next to the connector tube, build up 2 pillars that are 5 blocks high in front of the connector tube walls.

Add 2 rows of quartz block between the top 2 blocks of the pillars you built in step 23.

Above these, place a row of quartz 9 blocks long and then a row of quartz 7 blocks long, exactly as you did in step 21.

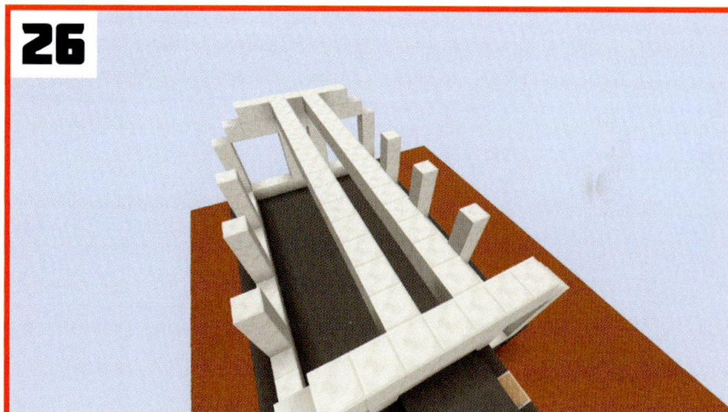

Add 2 rows of quartz running between the 2 middle pillars of the short walls.

Connect the long walls' pillars to the rows you added in step 25. Add 1 diagonal block and 2 horizontal blocks of quartz, as shown. This matches the shapes of the top corners of the short walls.

Finally, fill all the spaces between the pillars in with glass.

Add a row of stone slabs on the long sides of the greenhouse, above the cyan terracotta.

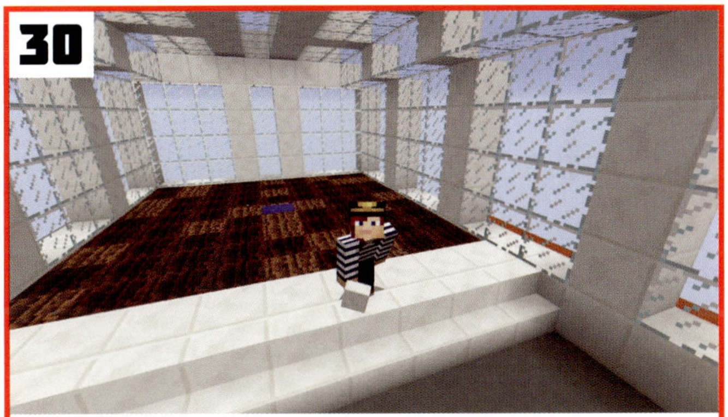

Add a 9x9 square of dirt to the inside of the greenhouse, against the wall farthest from the connector tube. Knock out the center block of this square and add a bucket of water. In front of this, add a row of quartz blocks and a row of quartz stairs. Plant your favorite veggies and enjoy your stay on Mars!

11. PIXEL ART DIAMOND PICK

Minecraft pixel art is the creation of two-dimensional (2D) pictures using blocks to represent each pixel.

A pixel is the smallest unit of an electronic image. You can create pixel art of Minecraft's items and objects pretty easily because these images are already created in a boxy, pixelated way. When you open up your inventory, you can see items displayed this way in sizes 16x16 pixels or smaller. These are perfect to copy for your first pixel art. To copy this axe and other images, you use a Minecraft block in place of each pixel. (You could make your pixel art really big by using 4 blocks for each pixel!)

You can also take other images and divide them into small squares to use for pixel art. Images that do not have a lot of details or are already small work best as pixel art. Each square that you divide the image into should be able to be represented by just one color.

MATERIALS

22 cyan wool
15 diamond blocks
11 oak wood planks
10 spruce wood planks
10 dark oak planks

Substitutions: You can use cyan concrete in place of the cyan wool and light blue concrete in place of the diamond block.

1

For this pixel art, we've chosen the diamond pick icon that you see in your Minecraft inventory. To get this image into a separate file, I've taken a screenshot by pressing F2. You can find a folder with your screenshots in your Minecraft folder.

2

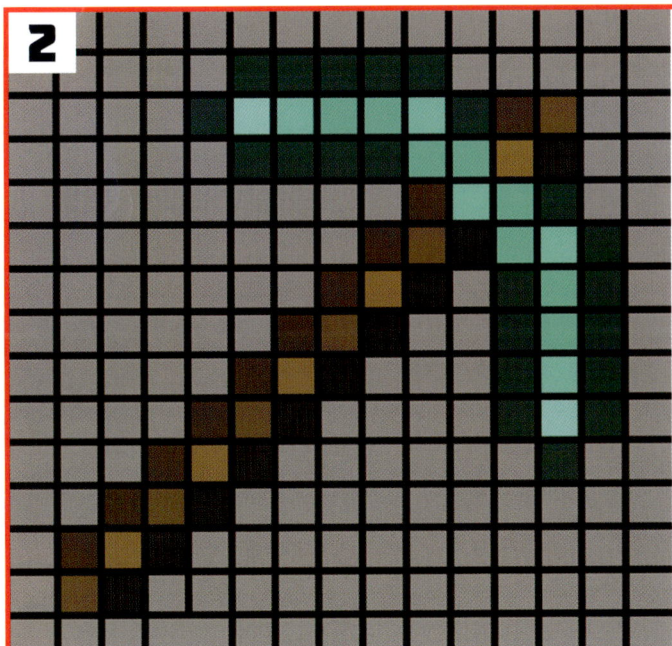

You can use an image editor program, like Windows Paint or the Mac's Preview function, to crop out the parts of your image you don't need and add grid lines that show each square. With a pixelated image like a Minecraft icon, you may not need grid lines, but they can still help with counting. This is your source image. Use this image to figure out which blocks you can use for each color and how many you will need. For this image, we can use dark oak planks for the dark bottom edge of the handle and spruce planks for the top edge. Then, although there are two colors used in the middle of the handle, they are pretty similar. Birch planks are too light, and acacia planks too orange, so we'll just use one block: oak wood planks. There are four colors in the icon for the diamond pick, the dark turquoise and three very similar shades of lighter turquoise. Because there aren't this many shades in Minecraft for turquoise, we'll just use two colors, one for the light and one for the dark: diamond blocks and cyan wool, respectively.

Place 9 dark wood planks in a diagonal line for the bottom edge of the handle.

Place 9 oak wood planks in a diagonal line next to the dark oak planks.

Now place 9 spruce wood planks in a diagonal line above the oak wood planks.

Place 5 diamond blocks around the top part of the handle, as shown.

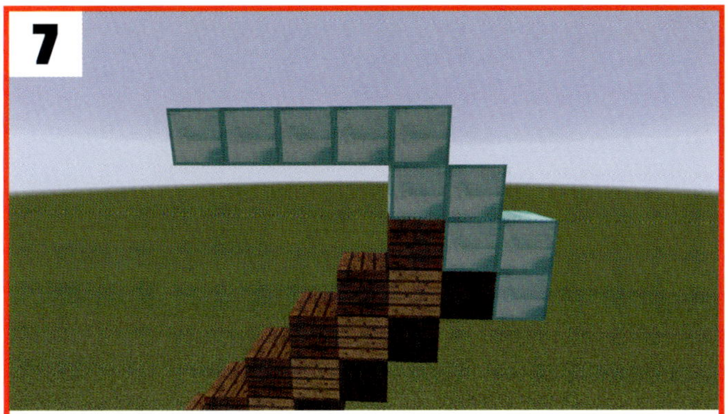

Above the top diamond block you just placed in step 6, place a row of 5 diamond blocks.

Next to the lowest diamond block placed in step 7, place a column of 5 diamond blocks.

Place cyan wool blocks around the diamond blocks, as shown.

Finish off the handle by placing 1 spruce plank, 1 dark oak plank, and 2 oak wood planks, as shown. Pixel art complete!

12. MASSIVE CREEPER

You can take your creativity to a new level by creating this wool creeper.

Even if you know it's made of wool, this massive creeper can still give you a sudden jolt of fear when you or an unsuspecting player catches sight of it. The upside is that it won't explode if you get close. You do need massive amounts of wool, though.

MATERIALS

59 stacks lime-green wool*
15½ stacks white wool
11½ stacks light gray wool
96 black wool
64 green wool
48 gray wool

*This count assumes you will build the creeper first entirely out of the lime-green wool. If you use white and light gray wool as well as green as you go, you'll only need about half of this amount.

Substitutions: Use similarly colored concrete instead of wool.

1

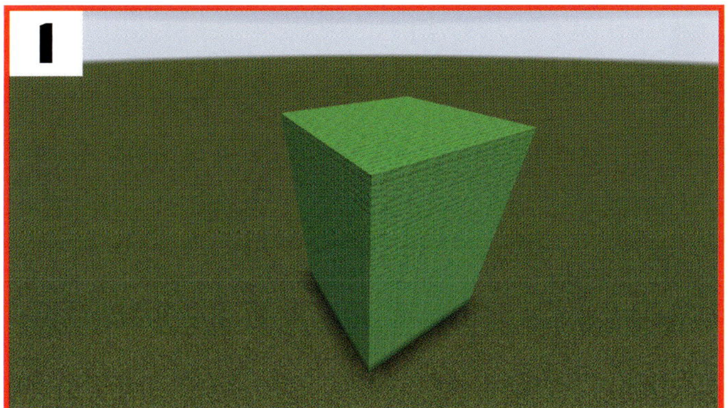

Build the right front foot of the creeper (left as you look at it) as a hollow cuboid with lime-green wool. It is 8x8 around and 12 blocks high.

2

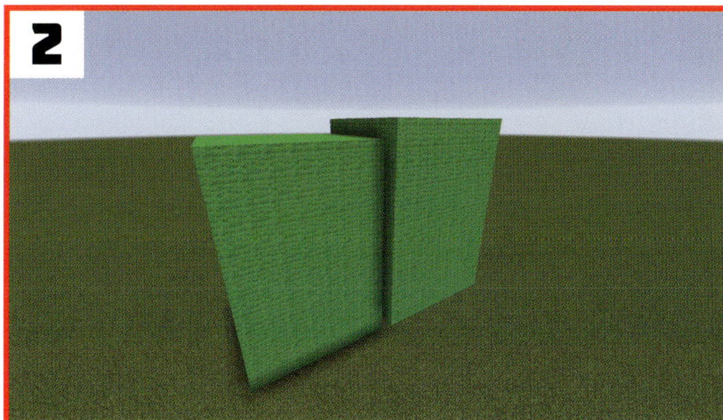

Build an identical left foot, but align it 1 block above and 1 block in front of the right foot. Offsetting the feet like this will make it look like the creeper is stepping forward.

3

Build the back right foot of the creeper at the same size, leaving 9 blocks between it and the front right foot. Position this foot up a block as you did with the front right foot.

4

Build the back left foot on the ground and aligned 1 block in front of the back right foot.

5

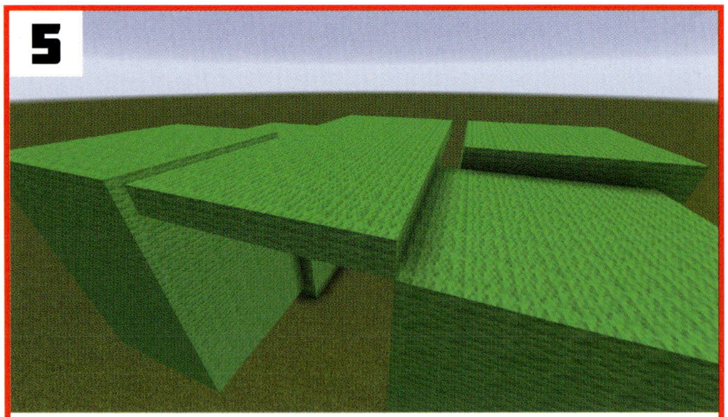

Build the base of the creeper's body with lime-green wool 8 blocks deep and 16 blocks wide. This base is a block up from the right front and left back feet.

6

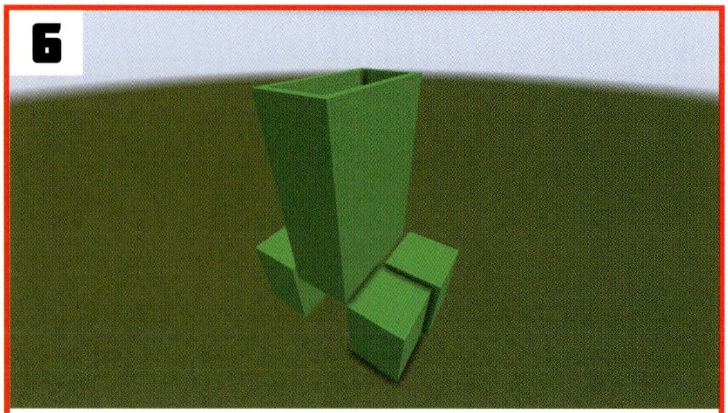

Build up walls on the body so it is 24 blocks high.

7

Fill in the gap between the body and the back right and front left feet with a row of wool.

8

On top of the body, build the base for the head. It extends 4 blocks out from the front and back walls of the body and is 16 blocks deep and 16 wide.

9

Add walls to the base of the head and build these up so they are 16 blocks high. Fill in the roof of the head.

10

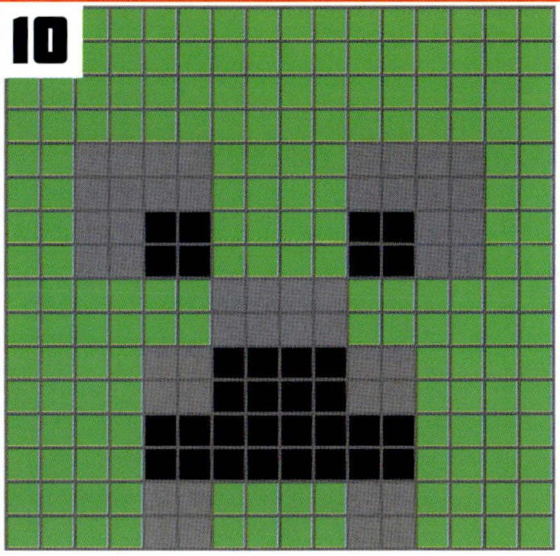

Creeper Face

Use the diagram to make the creeper's eyes and mouth from black wool and gray (the darker gray) wool.

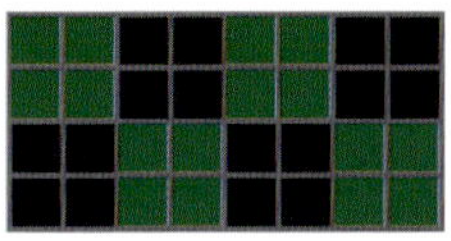

Creeper Toes

11

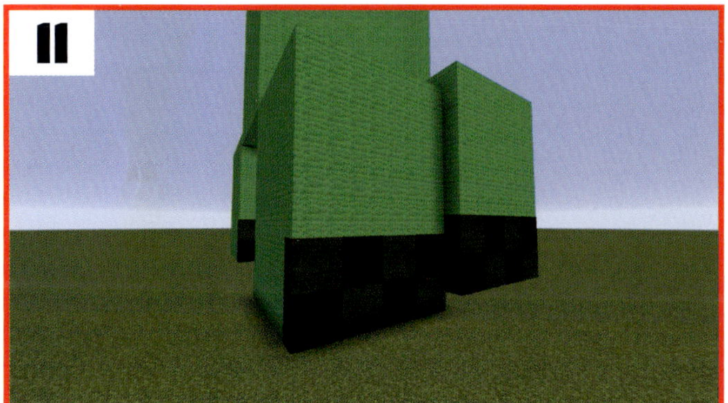

Use the diagram to make the creeper's toes at the bottom front of each foot using green and black wool.

12

Finally, it is time to add the splotches to the creeper's skin. Replace random, small patches, streaks, and single blocks of lime-green wool with white wool and light gray wool. Creeper complete.

13. CUPCAKE BAKERY

There may be lots of ways to build a bakery in Minecraft, but this one is extra special.

I can think of no better place to store and trade your cakes, pies, and cookies than a bakery shaped like the best type of cake, a chocolate cupcake! If you disagree about the flavor, you can tweak this design to make a vanilla or strawberry cupcake or a blueberry muffin.

MATERIALS

3½ stacks brown wool
2½ stacks pink wool
98 white wool
36 blue wool
6 pink stained glass panes
40 carpet (red, purple, brown, yellow, orange, and lime green)
1 dark oak wood door
1 Nether brick fence
For interior decoration: pumpkin pies, cookies, bread, cakes, item frames, End rods for lighting, birch wood stairs and slabs for counters, 9 pink carpet

Substitutions: In place of the wool, you can use colored concrete. In place of End rods for lighting, use torches or glowstone.

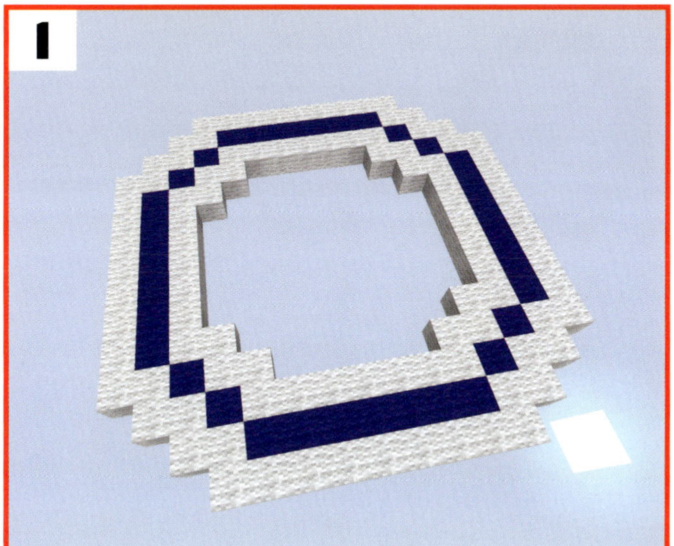

First make a plate for the cupcake to sit on. (If you don't want a plate, skip to step 2). Create the outline of the plate with white wool. It's a circle with sides 8 blocks long and 2 diagonal blocks between each side. Add a strip of blue wool blocks inside the plate's edge. Add another strip of white wool as shown.

Fill in the rest of the plate with brown wool. This will be the cupcake's base.

Add walls of brown wool above the outer blocks of the cupcake's base. Build them up to be 4 blocks high.

4

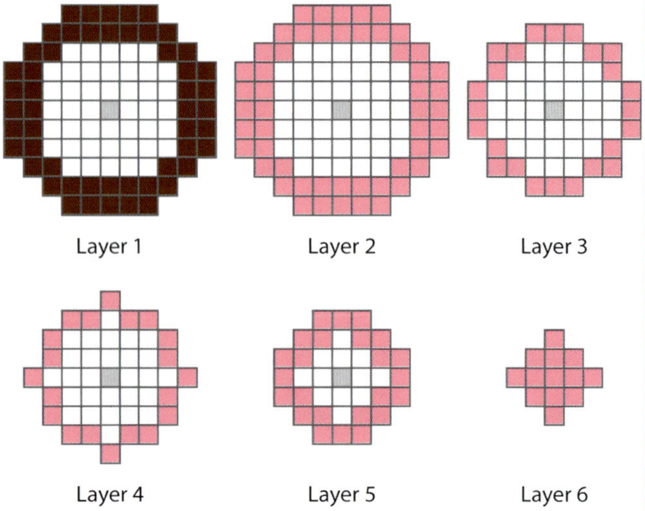

Above this, use the diagram to create the first layer, layer 1, of the roof using brown wool.

5

Using pink wool as icing, add the top 5 layers of the roof. Follow the grid diagram for each layer, from layer 2 to 6. Layer 2 is exactly the same as layer 1.

6

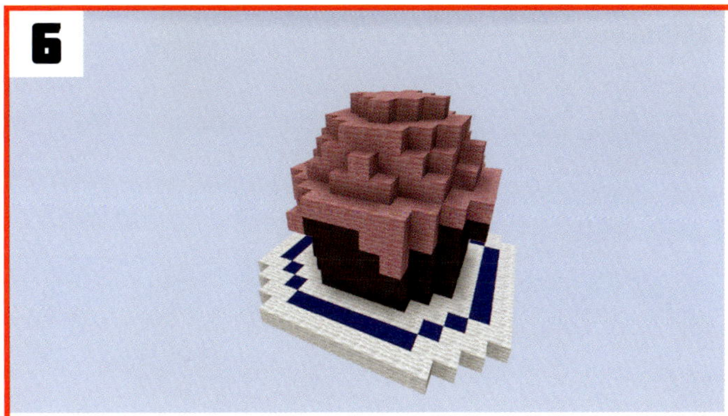

To make the icing goop a little, replace a few of the brown wool blocks beneath the icing with pink wool. Add extra pink wool below these to make a few drips.

7

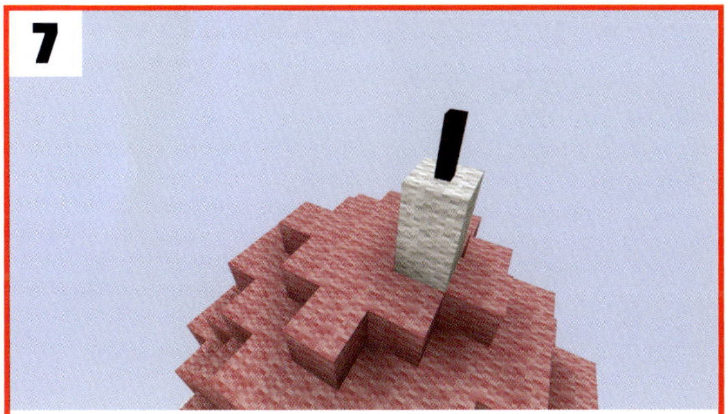

For a candle, add 2 blocks of white wool and a single Nether brick fence to the top of the icing.

8

Sprinkles! Add about 40 colored wool carpet randomly on top of the pink wool icing. Here I've used red, brown, yellow, purple, and lime-green carpet.

9

To the front of your bakery, add a dark oak wood door and 2 small pink stained glass pane windows.

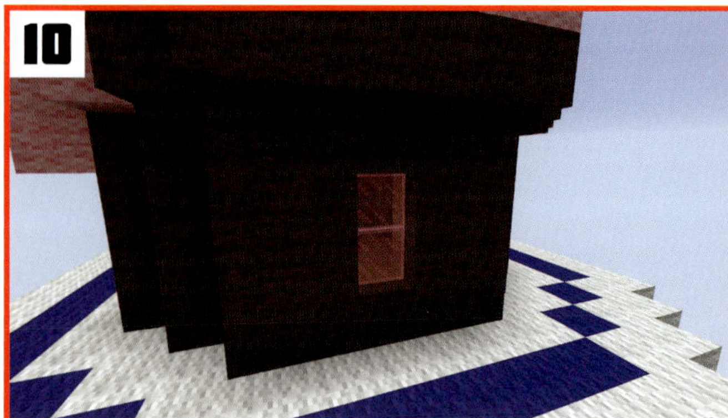

10

Add 2-pane high windows to the left and right sides of the bakery.

11

Inside, you can make counters with upside-down birch wood stairs and planks and load these with cakes. Add carpet for more color. In item frames you can place bread, pumpkin pie, cakes, and cookies. If you have them, use End rods for lights.

14. HAUNTED HOUSE

It's fun for Halloween but stands the test of any season in Minecraft.

With skeletons, creepers, zombies, and witches, not to mention pumpkins and jack-o'-lanterns, Minecraft is primed for a good old Halloween-style haunted house. Sagging porch, rotten walls, cobwebs, and broken windows? Check. Will there be a witch inside? You decide!

MATERIALS (house only)

4½ stacks oak wood planks
5 oak stairs
14 oak slabs*
28 oak wood fence (more if you'll be imprisoning mobs inside!)
1½ stacks spruce wood planks
17 spruce wood slabs*
43 spruce wood stairs
5 birch wood planks*
15 jungle wood planks*
6 jungle wood fences*
9 dark oak stairs*
2 dark oak slabs*
22 cobblestone
5 mossy cobblestone*
5 gravel*
20 cobwebs*
4 black stained glass panes
10 gray stained glass panes
4 ladders

*approximate

For the foundation of the house, build a 5x5 square of oak wood planks surrounded by cobblestone blocks.

Using oak wood planks, build the walls of the first floor 4 blocks high on top of the foundation. Fill in the top of the walls with oak wood planks.

Add a second floor that is also 4 blocks high, but indented 1 block from the front. Fill in the top with oak wood planks.

4

Add a third floor that is 4 blocks high and indented from each side by 1 block and fill in the top.

5

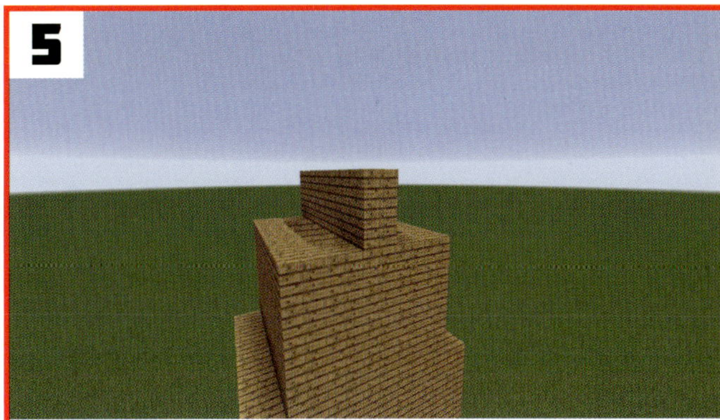

Run 2 rows of oak wood planks above this floor from the front of the house to the back.

6

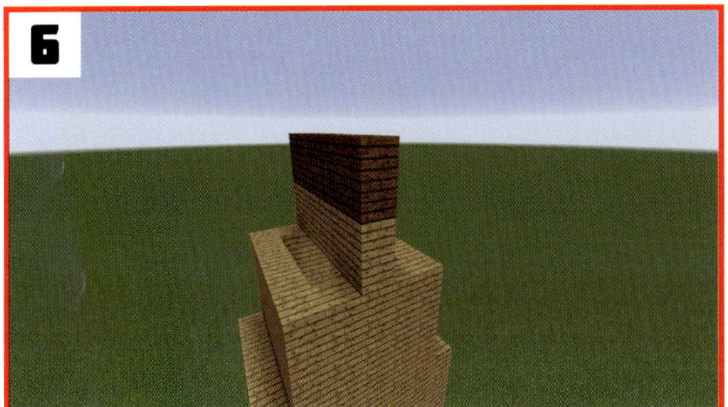

Add 2 rows of spruce wood, one on top of each other, on top of this last floor for the top of the roof.

7

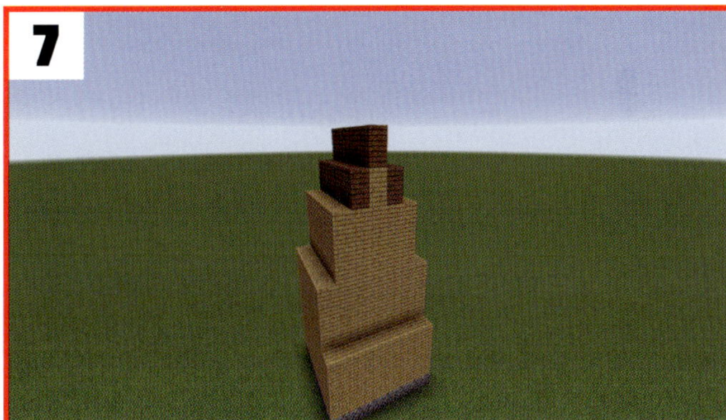

On either side of the oak wood rows you placed in step 6, add 2 rows of spruce wood planks for the next level down of the roof.

8

Below these rows, replace 2 rows of the oak wood walls with 2 rows of spruce wood planks. Do this on both sides of the roof.

9

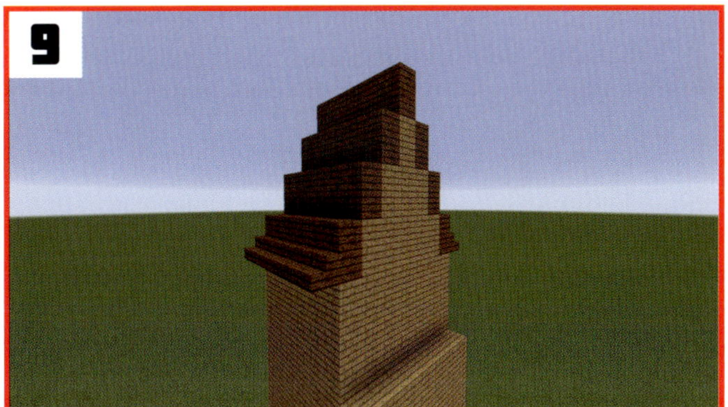

Below this, add 2 more rows of spruce wood planks for the roof on either side. Along the outside of the bottom row of the spruce roof, add a row of spruce stairs.

10

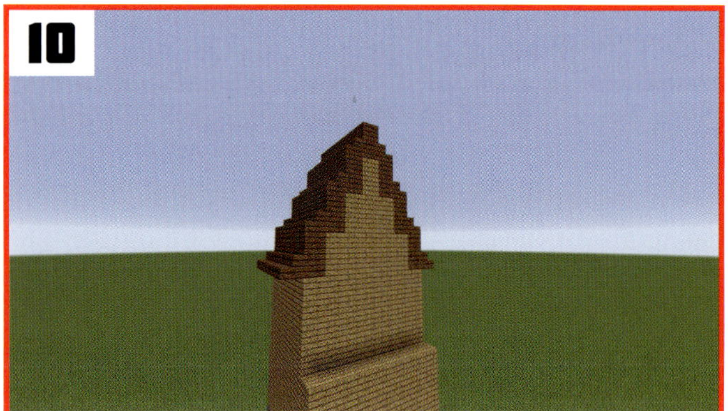

At each flat level of the roof except the top, add a row of spruce stairs.

11

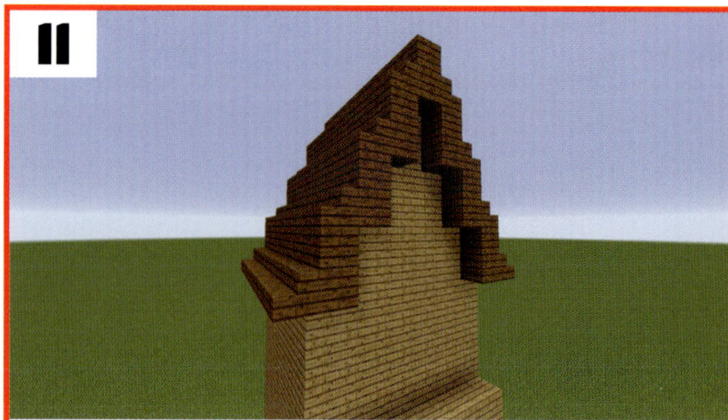

Now, using spruce stairs and planks, extend the roof out 1 block in front and in back of the house.

12

To create the front porch, first add 3 oak wood planks at the front of the house, as shown.

13

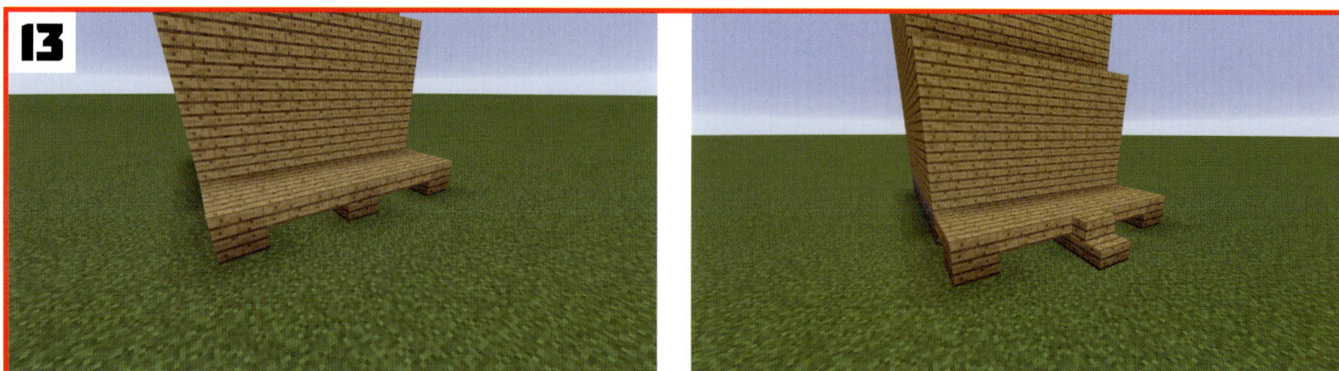

Add oak wood slabs as shown to fill out the floor of the porch. Add an oak wood stair in the center.

14

For the porch roof, first add a row of spruce wood slabs at the same level as the second floor.

15

Add a second row of spruce wood slabs a half block below the row in step 14.

16

Use oak wood fence for the railing and support.

17

Add a spruce wood door to the front wall and break holes for windows that are 2 blocks high on either side.

18

Add a row of oak wood fences above the porch roof and add 3 open windows, 2 blocks high, for the second floor.

19

On the third floor, add an open window 3 blocks high.

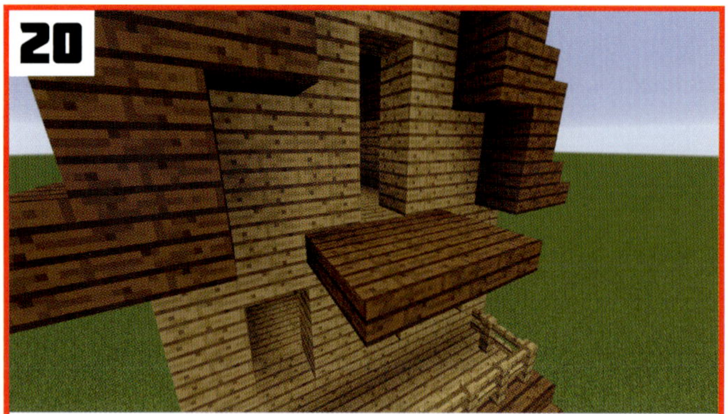

Outside of this window, add a porch of spruce wood slabs that is 3x2.

Add oak wood fence as a railing.

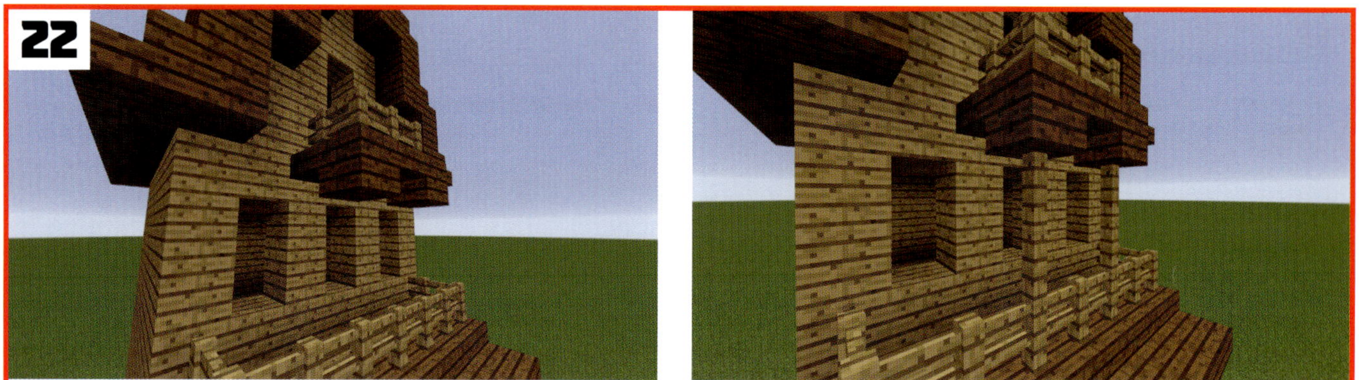

Add 2 spruce slabs at the outer corners of this porch, underneath it. Connect these to the railings below with oak wood fence.

On both sides of the house, add 2 open windows 2 blocks high, one on each floor.

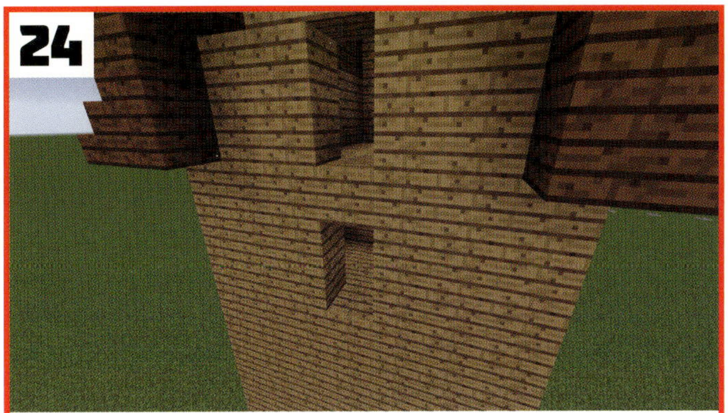

On the back wall of the house, add an open window, 2 blocks high, for the second floor and another, 3 blocks high, for the third floor.

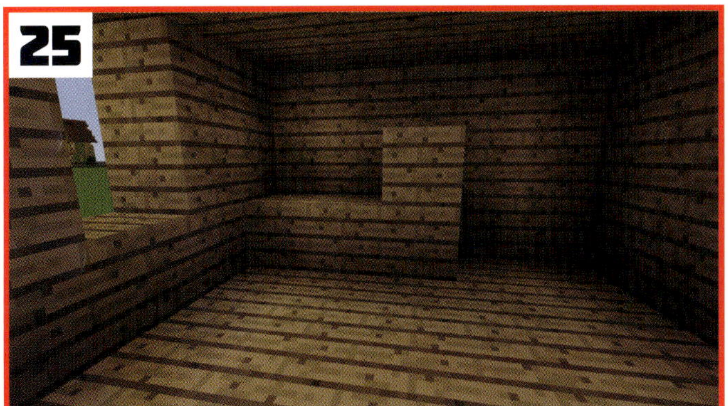

Inside, create the base for the stairs to the second floor using 4 oak wood planks in a sideways L shape, as shown.

Add 4 oak wood stairs to the base to finish the stairs. Break blocks in the floor above so you can reach the second floor. (The fourth stair is hidden in this screenshot; it is at the same level as the second floor.)

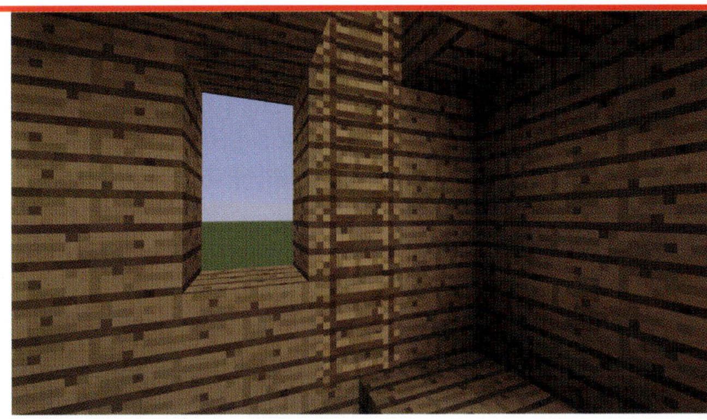

To get to the third floor, break the block in the ceiling above the last stair you placed in step 26 and add ladders.

28

Now that the house structure is complete, it's time to add details. Replace some of the cobblestone foundation with mossy cobblestone and a few gravel. For a moldy, rotten look, replace oak wood planks in the floors and walls with small patches of jungle wood planks. Replace some of the oak fences with jungle fences as well. For a "cheap repair" look, replace some oak wood planks with a few patches of birch wood planks.

29

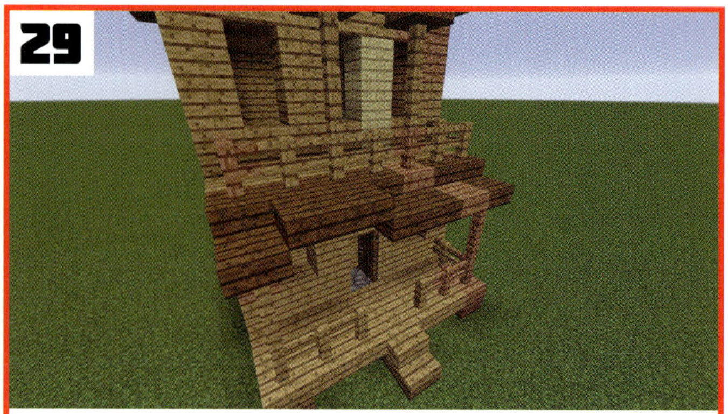

Warp the roof of the bottom porch by moving a few spruce slabs up a half block. Add some moldiness by replacing a couple slabs with jungle wood.

30

Warp and break the roof of the house by replacing some spruce stairs with dark oak wood stairs and dark oak wood and spruce slabs. Break a couple stairs while you're at it!

31

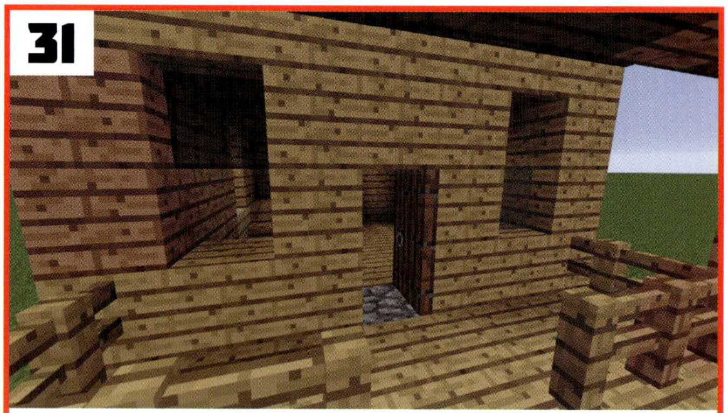

Add single panes of black and gray glass to the windows to make them look like they've been broken.

32

Add a few vines and some cobwebs. To stop a vine from growing, you can block its path down with string.

33

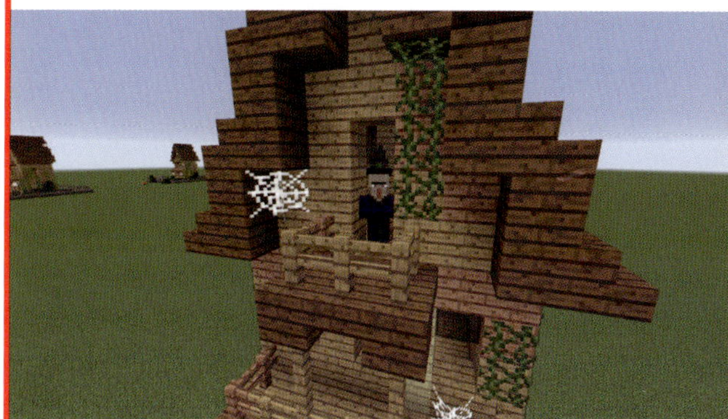

If you play in creative mode, you can add skeletons, zombies, witches, and creepers pretty safely using spawn eggs. Make sure to spawn these mobs in the fenced-off areas inside.

34

Use landscaping to make your haunted house even creepier. You can make a worn-out path with gravel and mossy cobblestone. Add a surrounding wall made of cracked and mossy brick, mossy cobblestone, and gravel topped with iron bars. Add patches of podzol and coarse dirt to the garden. Finally, add spruce leaf blocks, vines, and dead bushes for an overgrown mess.

15. SECRET WISHING WELL

Not every building in Minecraft needs to have a purpose, like storage or trading or protection.

This secret, overgrown garden in a forest with a wishing well is a nice place just to walk through or pass by. Throughout the build, use a few mossy stone bricks and cracked stone bricks in place of regular stone bricks for a weathered look. Do the same with the cobblestone blocks and walls: replace a few with mossy cobblestone.

MATERIALS*

2 stacks cobblestone and mossy cobblestone walls
2 stacks cobblestone and mossy cobblestone
16 stone bricks (total includes mossy stone bricks and cracked stone bricks)
20 stone brick stairs
4 stone brick slabs
5 gravel
4 glowstone blocks
2 buckets of water
10 vines
4 oak saplings
50 oak leaves
4 iron bars
Bonemeal to grow grass and flowers

*includes approximate amounts for the wall and landscaping, too

Deep in a forest, clear out a lot about 27 blocks by 27 blocks.

In the center of the lot, replace grass with 4 mossy stone bricks in a square. This is the base of the well. Add 4 sides to the well using stone bricks, as shown.

Add a second layer of stone bricks to the first, as shown. For a weathered look, use 2 or 3 mossy stone bricks or cracked stone bricks.

Encircle the bottom of the well with stone brick stairs.

5

At each corner of the well, add cobblestone walls mixed with mossy cobblestone walls 3 blocks high.

6

Add 1 stone brick slab on top of each pillar.

7

On each side of the well, in between the slabs, add 2 blocks of stone bricks. You can add a couple mossy stone bricks and a cracked stone brick here as well.

8

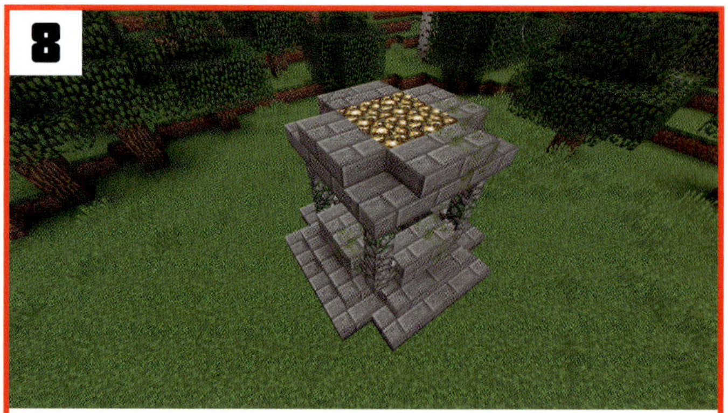

In the empty square left inside the stone bricks, add 4 glowstone blocks.

Above the glowstone, add 2 stone brick blocks and 2 mossy or cracked stone bricks.

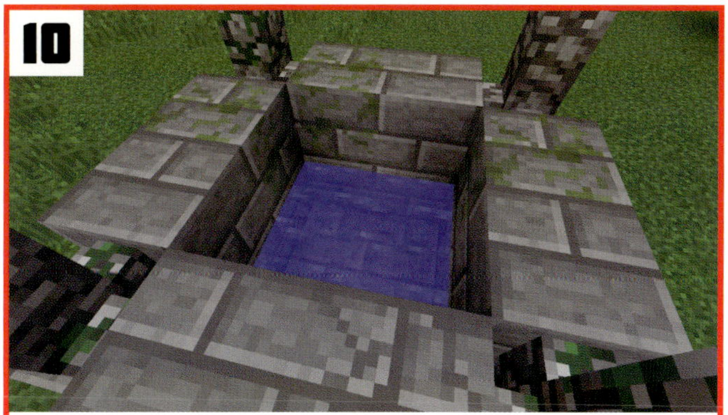

Place 2 buckets of water inside the well, diagonally to each other. This should fill up the bottom layer of the well.

Add 3 or 4 vines to the bottom and roof of the well.

Add the base of a wall that weaves, not quite straight, around the wishing well. Leave 6 or more blocks between the wishing well and the wall.

For the entrance of the wishing well garden, leave a space of 2 blocks. On each side, add a second cobblestone block. Above these add a row of 4 cobblestone walls.

For a gate that's been opened and broken, place 2 iron bars on the inside of one side of the entrance. Place 2 more iron bars next to these on the outside of the entrance.

Finish off the walls by adding cobblestone and mossy cobblestone walls above the cobblestone blocks. You can make your wall look even more weathered by replacing a few of the bottom cobblestone blocks with walls and with just a couple andesite blocks and/or gravel.

Now make an overgrown path from the garden entrance to your well. Use a few gravel, a few mossy cobblestone, and a few regular cobblestone.

17

Landscape your secret garden. Add an extra tree or two. For mini trees, place a single log with 4 leaf blocks around it and another on top. Use oak, spruce, and birch leaves to make overgrown bushes along the walls and creeping around the well. Place a few vines on your bushes and walls. (Too many can overtake the look, so add maybe 7 to 10 vines). Use bone meal to grow grass and flowers and plant other flowers like rose bushes and lilacs if you like. Use bone meal on grass to make it double tall. Add ferns and use bone meal on some of these to make them double tall.

MAKING GIANT OAKS

To make a giant oak, place a column of glass blocks 4 or 5 blocks high next to your oak sapling. Bone meal the sapling—you may need to do this 10 or more times—to get your giant oak.

16. CAR

Even if you haven't reached driving age, you can create a car in Minecraft.

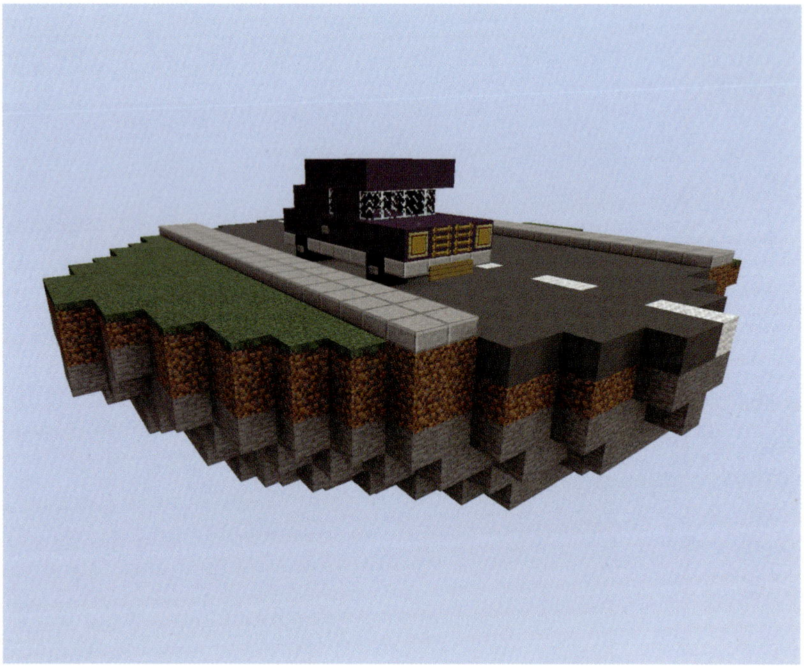

If you are building a modern city or house, cars are great details to add. You can design different types of cars using the same base and elements as this car, just adding different colors, fronts, backs, and windows.

MATERIALS

54 blue terracotta
24 stone slabs
4 black wool
6 stone buttons
4 signs
2 fences
4 item frames
2 glass blocks
2 yellow stained glass blocks
6 glass panes
2 red stained glass panes

Substitutions: Use any color terracotta or cement for the car body.

First, create the 2 front wheels of the car. Place 2 blocks of black wool with 2 empty blocks between them.

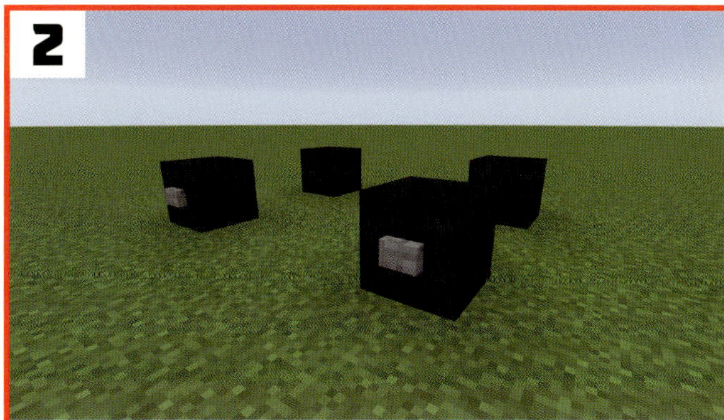

Now create the 2 back wheels. Leave 3 empty blocks between these and the front wheels. Put stone buttons on the outer sides of each wheel.

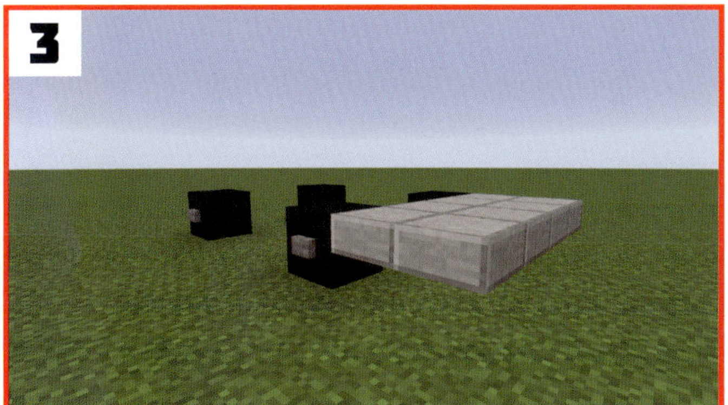

For the undercarriage, use stone slabs at the same height as the wheels. Place 2 rows of 4 in front of the 2 front wheels.

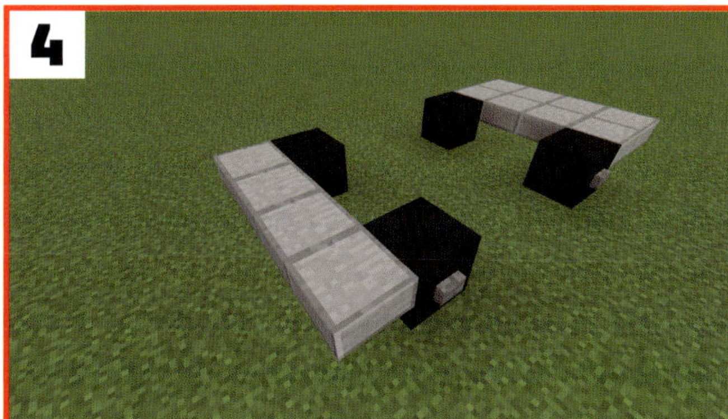

Behind the back wheels, place 1 row of 4 stone slabs.

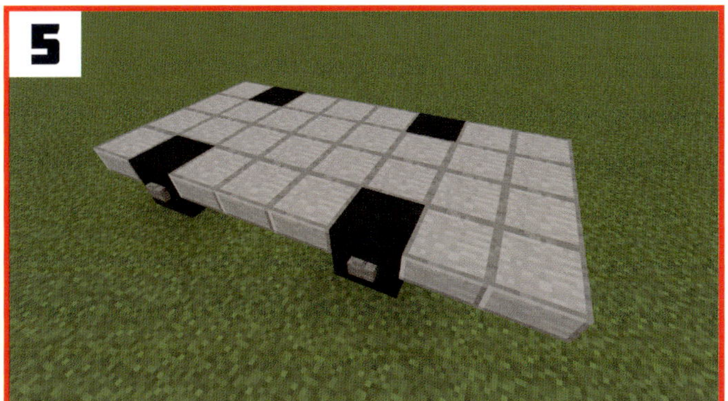

Now fill in the space between the front and back rows of slabs with more stone slabs.

Place 1 layer of blue terracotta blocks above the layer of stone slabs.

7

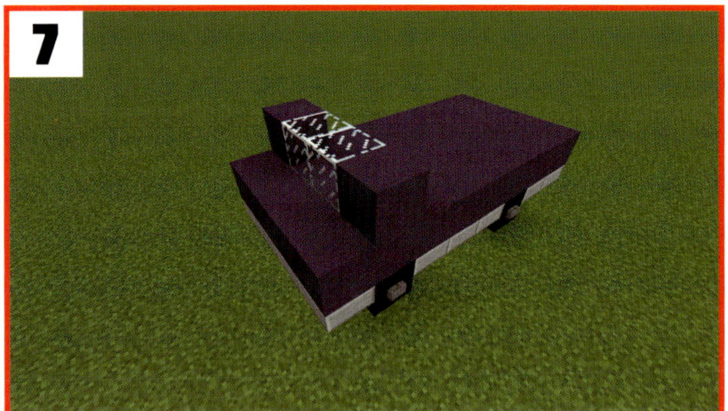

For the back window, place 2 blue terracotta blocks and 2 glass blocks as shown, 1 block away from the back of the car.

8

Place a column of blue terracotta 2 blocks high in front of the back window, on either side of the car, as shown.

9

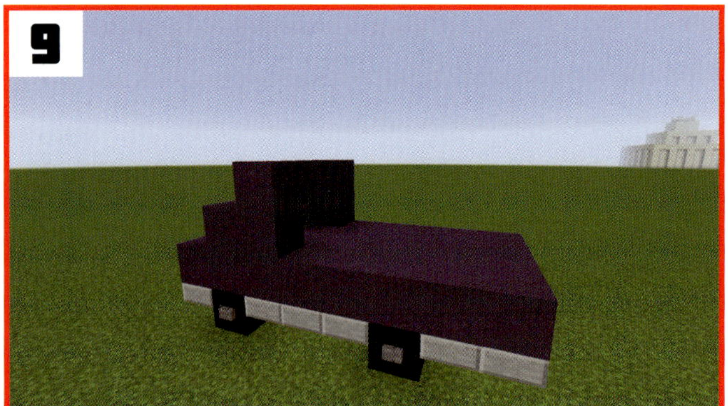

Use 2 more blue terracotta blocks to join the 2 columns.

10

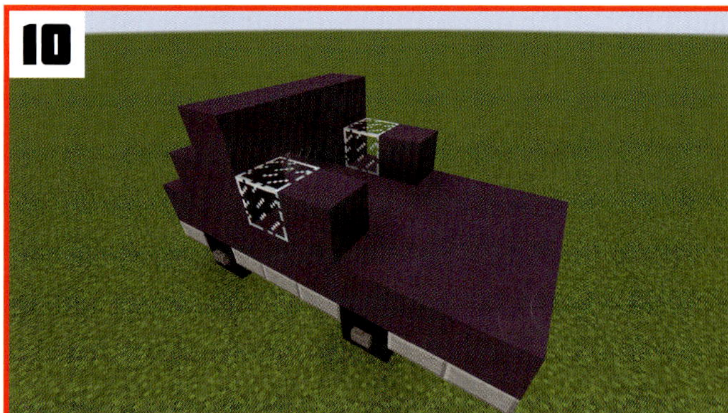

In front of each of these blocks, place a glass block (as the side window) and another blue terracotta block on either side of the car.

11

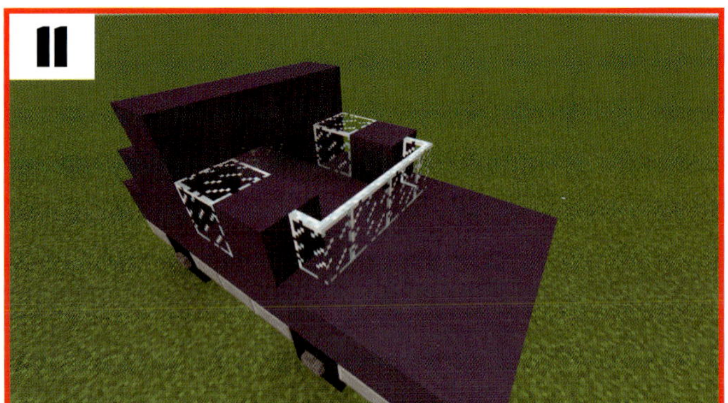

In front of the last 2 terracotta blocks, place a row of 4 glass panes for the front windscreen, as shown.

12

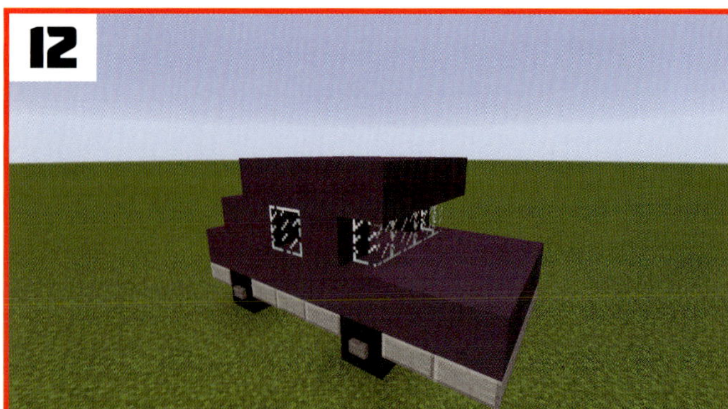

Place 3 more 4-block rows of blue terracotta as the top of the car, as shown.

13

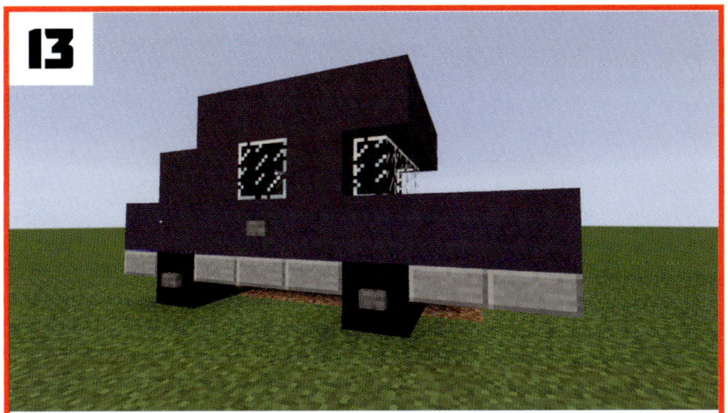

Add stone buttons beneath each side window for door handles.

14

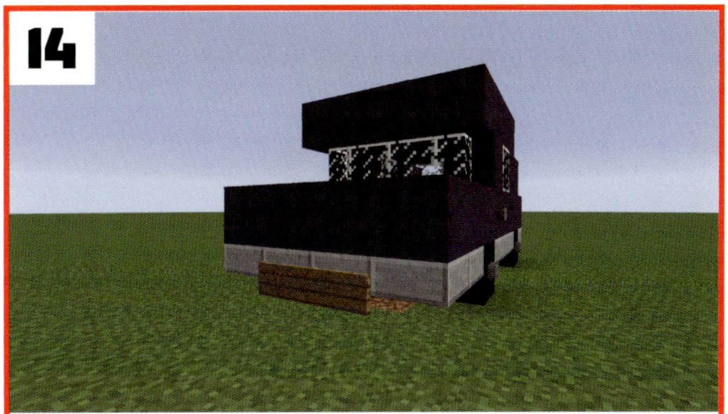

At the front and back of the car, add 2 signs on the 2 center stone slabs for license plates.

15

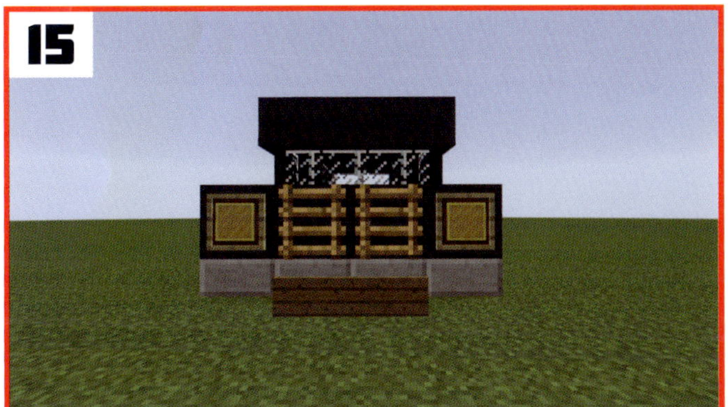

On the front, above the signs, place 2 ladders for the grill. On either side of the grill, add 2 item frames. Place a yellow stained glass pane in each to make headlights.

16

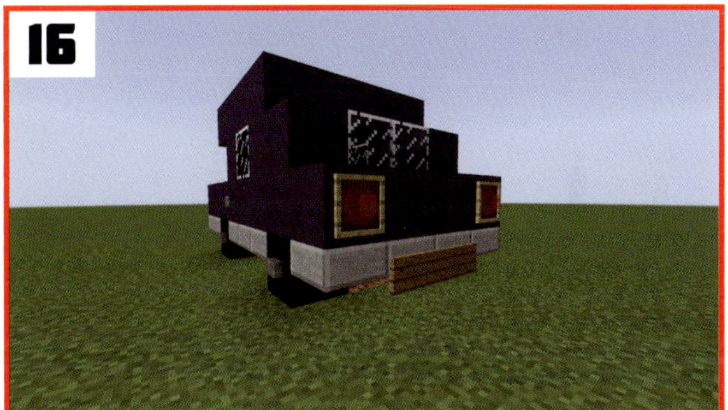

On the back, do the same to create taillights, but use red glass blocks instead of panes. Your car is ready to drive! Oh, wait.

17. GINGERBREAD HOUSE

Is one building of cake enough?

We can make pretend little houses of gingerbread in real life, so we might as well make some more in Minecraft. Yum. We can make houses of carrots and broccoli later.

MATERIALS

5½ stacks brown wool
1½ stacks white wool
72 purple wool
15 red wool
12 lime-green wool
5 magenta wool
5 yellow wool
5 orange wool
13 brightly colored glass panes (orange, yellow, lime green, purple, magenta)
1 dark oak wood door
8½ stacks snow blocks

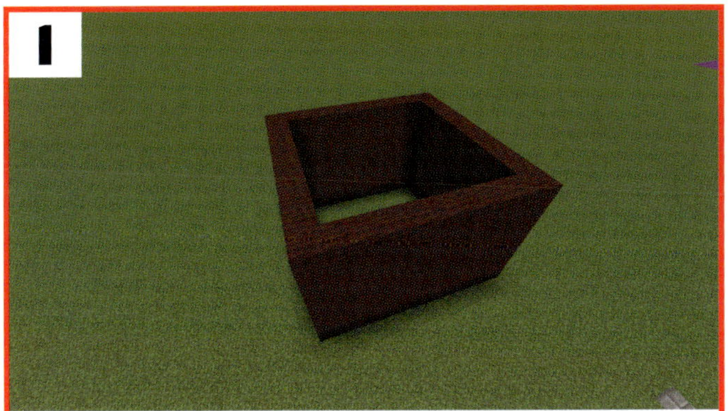

First let's build the structure of the house. Start with a 9x9 square of brown wool that is 6 blocks high.

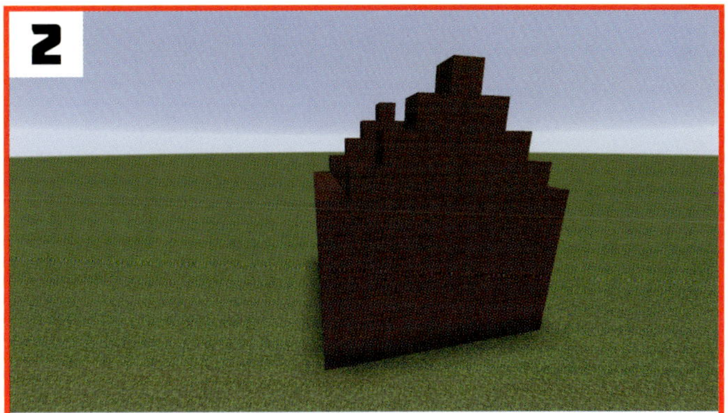

Start the roof. Add a triangle of brown wool to the front and back walls that is 4 blocks high and indented 1 block in from the side walls.

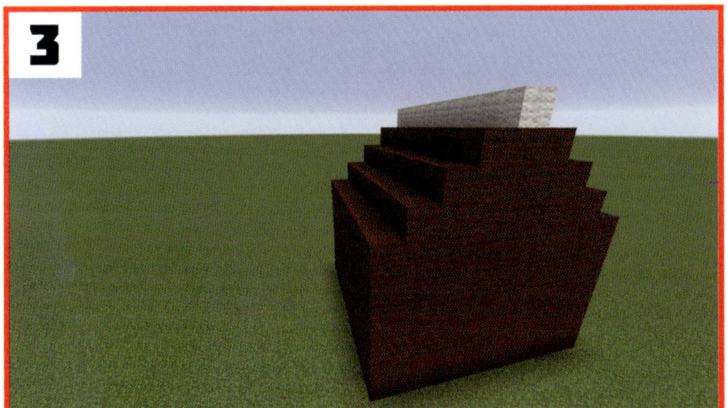

Run rows of brown wool from the back triangle to the front triangle. Make the very top row out of white wool.

Replace the top brown wool blocks along the outside edges of the roof with white wool, as shown.

Add a row of white wool on the left and right sides of the roof, as shown.

Extend the front and back of the roof with 1 block of white wool at each level, as shown.

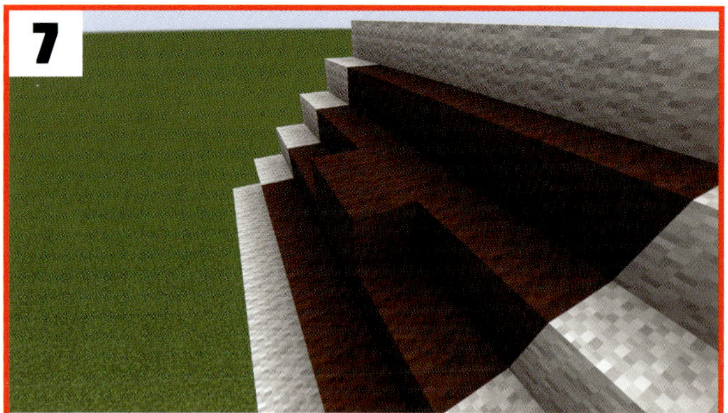

At the center of the roof on one side, add 2 brown wool blocks to make a 2x2 base for the chimney.

Build up the chimney walls with 4 more levels of brown wool. Add a last level of white wool at the top.

Break a gap for the entrance that is 2 blocks high and centered on the front wall. Use purple wool for your floor inside the house.

Add a frame of white wool outside of the doorway.

Add a dark oak wood door inside the white wool frame.

Above the door, break a single block, centered between the door and the roof, as shown.

13

Add a frame of white wool blocks to the window, and add a single lime-green pane of glass.

14

Add windows that are 2 blocks high on either side of the door and fill them with colorful stained glass panes. Add a white wool block above each window for its frame.

15

Add 2 similar windows to the right and left sides of the house, using colorful glass panes and white wool for the frames.

16

Decorate the roof with different colored wool blocks as candy, using about 12 blocks on each side of the roof.

17

Now that your gingerbread house is done, add some landscaping. Here, I've added a wall of brown wool around the house and replaced the grass with snow blocks. I've also added lime-green "bushes" to the front corners of the house, candy canes made with red and white wool, and a wonky bright purple path.

18. FOUNTAIN

Fountains are a great way to liven up the outside of lots of different types of buildings in Minecraft.

To make them look really good, design them so that the water flows through the tiers rather than over every side. This way you can see the structure of the fountain itself. Just add holes in the bottom of the tiers to let water through and test to make sure the water is flowing the way you want.

MATERIALS

2 stacks stone bricks
53 stone brick stairs
16 stone brick slabs
9 cobblestone
75 cobblestone stairs
1 cobblestone wall
Buckets of water

1

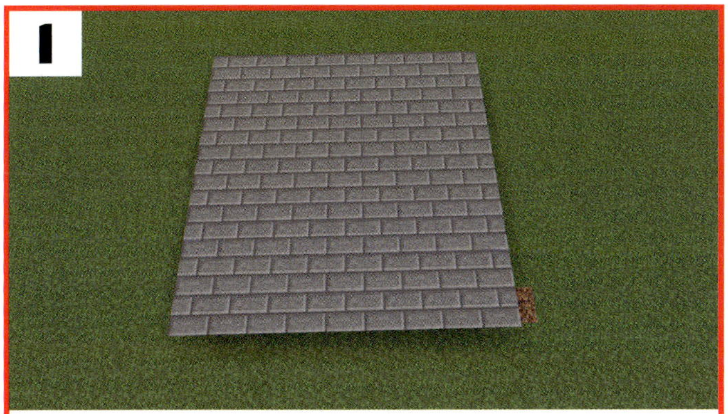

We'll start by building the fountain's basin. First, place stone bricks in a 9x9 square.

2

Add another row of 7 stone bricks along each side to create this Minecraft circle.

3

Add a cobblestone stair in the center of one of the base's sides.

4

Place stairs all around this base. Alternate between cobble and stone brick stairs.

5

One block in and above from the stairs you placed in step 4, place another circle of cobblestone and stone brick stairs.

6

Now build the central column of the fountain. In the center of the base, place 5 cobblestone in a cross shape.

7

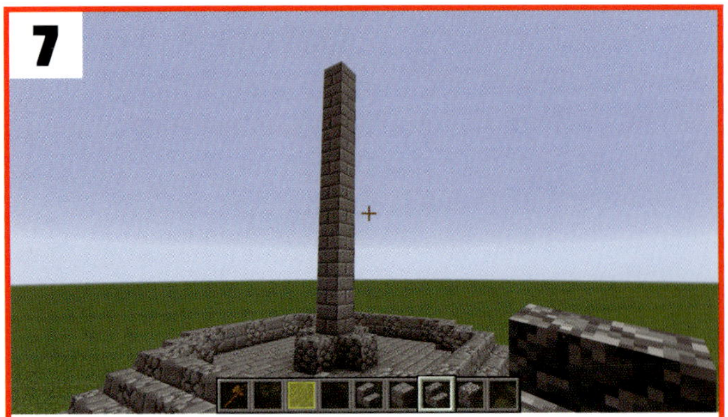

Above this cross, place a column of 11 stone brick blocks.

8

On top of each cobblestone block at the base of the column, place a cobblestone stair.

9

Now let's build the lower tier of the fountain. Three blocks above the stairs placed in step 8, place upside-down cobblestone stairs all around the column. This should leave a space of 2 blocks between these 2 sets of stairs.

10

Place stone brick blocks above the stairs placed in step 9.

11

On the center and bottom of each side of the square of stone bricks you placed in step 10, place a stone brick slab.

12

At each corner of the square of stone bricks, place another stone brick block diagonally.

13

On each of the 2 outer sides of each diagonal stone brick block, place an upside-down cobble stair.

14

On each side of the fountain, between the 2 upside-down cobble stairs, place 3 more upside-down stairs. Next to the cobblestone stairs use stone brick stairs, and in the middle use another cobblestone stair. This tier has 8 empty spaces for water to fall through.

Now let's build the upper tier of the fountain. Three blocks up on the column, place an upside-down stone brick stair on each side of the column. (There should be 2 blocks between these stairs and the stone brick blocks below.)

Above each of the stairs placed in step 15, place a full stone brick block. On the outermost side of these 4 blocks, place an upside-down cobblestone stair.

On top of the 4 stone brick blocks placed in step 16, place a regular cobblestone stair.

Above the upside-down stairs you placed in step 17, place a row of 3 stone slabs, as shown. Do this on each side of the tier.

19

Above the top stone brick block in the fountain's column, place a single cobblestone wall.

20

Fill in the bottom basin of the fountain with enough water blocks so that water is no longer flowing. You should be able to place 1 bucket every other block along each of the 4 sides and a few in the corners to create standing water.

21

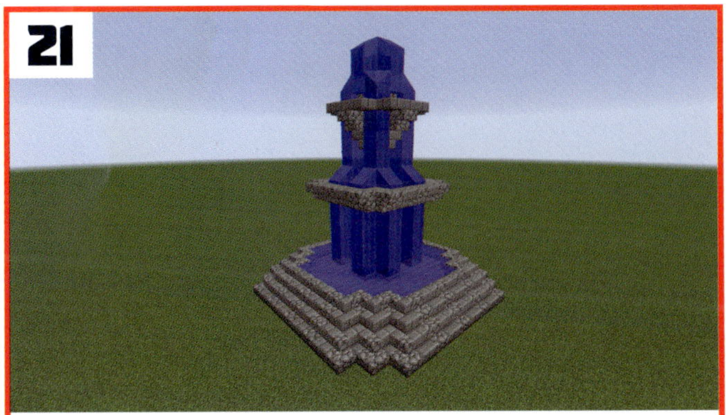

Finally, place a bucket of water on top of the cobblestone wall at the very top of the fountain.

19. JUNGLE TREE HIDEAWAY

Even if you can't build a treehouse in real life, you can have one in Minecraft.

This jungle tree hideaway would be perfect as a starter home or as a base for your parrot-taming quests.

MATERIALS

32 (½ stack) of jungle wood logs
64 (1 stack) jungle wood slabs
38 jungle wood planks
36 dark oak wood planks
35 dark oak wood stairs
13 dark oak wood fences
½ stack jungle leaves

Substitutions: Swap in any wood, although it will look best if you use contrasting woods (a lighter wood and a darker wood).

1

Plant or find yourself a 2x2 jungle tree that is about 30 blocks high.

2

Eight blocks down from the top canopy of leaves, build a 5x5 square of jungle wood planks. There should be 7 blocks of space between this floor and the bottom of the canopy.

3

Add 2 blocks to each corner and place dark oak fences along the front and sides of the platform.

4

Start the roof. Place 2 rows of dark oak planks along either side of the house, as shown. These extend 1 block beyond the front wall.

5

Add a row of dark oak stairs above the row of dark oak planks on each side.

6

Add 2 more rows of dark oak planks diagonal to the stairs.

7

Add stairs above these rows as well.

8

Add a single row of dark oak planks between the 2 rows of stairs.

9

Add a single row of dark oak slabs right above the last row of planks.

10

At the front of the treehouse, add a row of 3 jungle wood planks between the lowest dark oak planks. Above these place 4 dark oak fences, as shown.

11

Finally, add 2 rows of dark oak stairs a block down from the lowest dark oak planks, along the sides of the walls. This step finishes the roof.

12

At the back of the treehouse, add a slab of jungle wood between the floor and the tree.

Place an acacia wood door on top of this slab.

Add jungle wood logs to finish the back of the treehouse.

Place jungle wood slabs as stairs spiraling down around the tree trunk.

16

Underneath the treehouse, between the stairs and the house platform, create tree branches to support the house. Use jungle wood logs that come out from the main trunk and go diagonally a few blocks and up to the platform.

17

Finally, add some more jungle oak log branches to your tree and some more jungle leaves, if you think it needs it. You've made a cozy jungle hideaway just big enough for your bed and a few important things.

20. PIGSTY

A home for farm animals is one of my favorite things to build in Minecraft, whether it's a stable, a cow shack, a chicken pen, or a pigsty.

Every farm animal can use a sweet home, some hay, and a nice green pasture with pleasant hills and ponds.

Throughout this build, use a few mossy stone bricks and cracked stone bricks in place of regular stone brick for a weathered look. Do the same with the cobblestone blocks and walls: replace a few with mossy cobblestone.

MATERIALS

32 bricks
6 brick stairs
14 dark oak wood planks
21 dark oak slabs
126 dark oak fences*
114 cobblestone*
1 cobblestone wall
For landscaping: coarse dirt, hay bales, sugarcane, oak leaves, oak logs, oak saplings, and bone meal

Substitutions: You can replace the bricks with stone bricks and the dark oak with any wood.

Clear an area about 25x25 for your pigsty. Wall in this area using cobblestone blocks with dark oak wood fences above, as shown. Make sure the walls take some zigzags here and there.

Leave a single block space in the wall for the pen entrance. In the ground, place a cobblestone wall. On top of this, place a single dark oak fence. This allows you to hop quickly over the dark oak fence.

Two or three blocks from one side of the pen, build the base of your pigsty using bricks. First, make a rectangle that is 7 blocks wide, 4 deep, and 1 block high, leaving 3 empty blocks at the front, as shown. These will be the pigs' entrances to the sty.

Place a row of 7 brick blocks on top of the front row.

5

Place a row of 7 brick blocks on top of the back row.

6

At each of the 2 back corners of the sty, place 2 brick blocks, 1 above the corner block and 1 in front of it.

7

In the center of the back wall, place 1 brick block.

8

On either side of this center brick block, place 2 upside-down brick stairs facing away from each other. This will leave 4 little square gaps that will help air flow in and out of the sty.

9

Now on each of the 2 sides of the sty, place upside-down brick stairs facing the back. These will be 2 little windows for the pigs, 1 on each side wall.

10

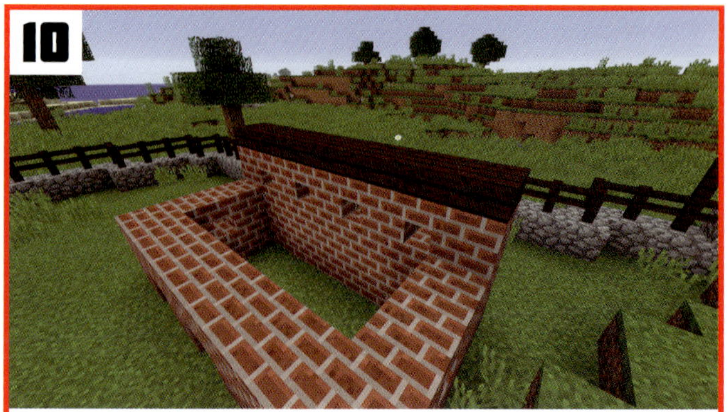

For the roof, first place a row of dark oak slabs above the back wall.

11

In front of this row, place 2 rows of dark oak planks.

12

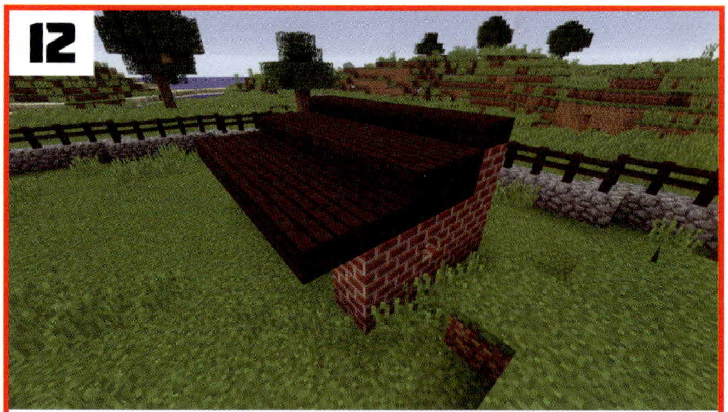

In front of the planks, place 2 rows of dark oak slabs.

Place dark oak fence gates in each of the 3 front sty entrances.

Add a small pond to your pen. First dig out the grass 1 block deep. Dig out about 25 blocks total in an irregular shape. Replace the blocks at the bottom of the pool with coarse dirt blocks.

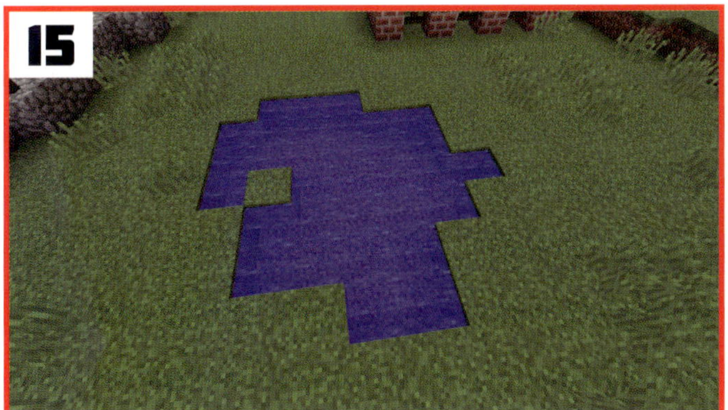

Fill in the pond with buckets of water.

Now for landscaping: Add an oak tree or two. For a tiny tree, place oak leaves on all sides and the top of a single oak log. Then create the most-trampled areas of the pen—areas that a farmer and pigs walk around on most, so grass has trouble growing. These would be from the gate to the sty and pond, around the front of the sty, and around the pond. Create these trampled areas with coarse dirt and path blocks in a messy pattern, leaving some grass blocks. (To create a path block, right-click a shovel on a grass block.) At the side of the sty, place hay bales in a clump. Add just a couple sugar cane around the pond. Use oak leaves to create bushes. (Make sure the leaves don't provide an escape route for your animals!) Use bone meal to add grass and double-tall grass. Finally, don't forget the pigs!

21. BARN

Why not make your animals feel at home?

This classic red barn is big enough for 8 horses or other farm animals and a whole ton of storage. You really could live in it too, although you'd want to close off the door area.

MATERIALS

12 stacks red terracotta
12 stacks quartz blocks
1½ stacks spruce wood logs
6 stacks spruce wood planks
3½ stacks stone bricks
16 quartz stairs
29 glass panes
81 spruce wood fences
8 spruce wood fence gates
8 ladders

Substitutions: Use red and white concrete in place of the red terracotta and quartz. You also could use different types of contrasting wood for the barn and stone bricks for the roof.

1

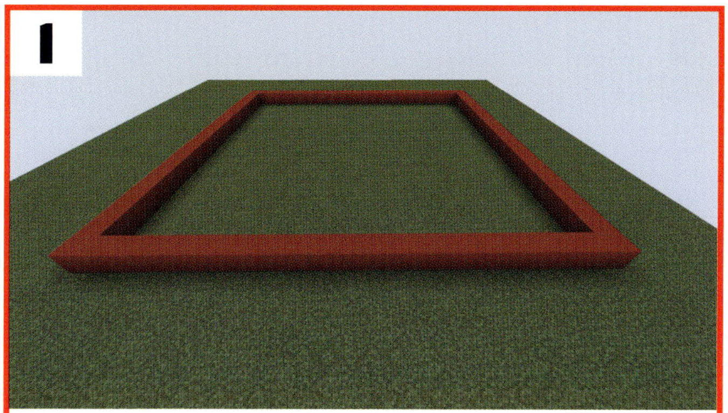

Build a 21x21 square of red terracotta.

2

Build up the walls to be 7 blocks high.

3

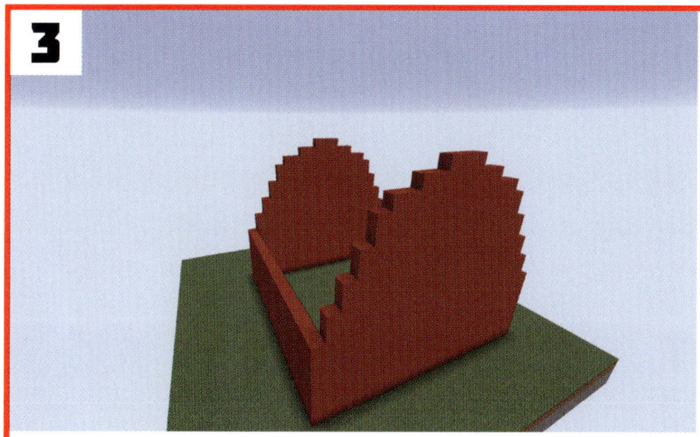

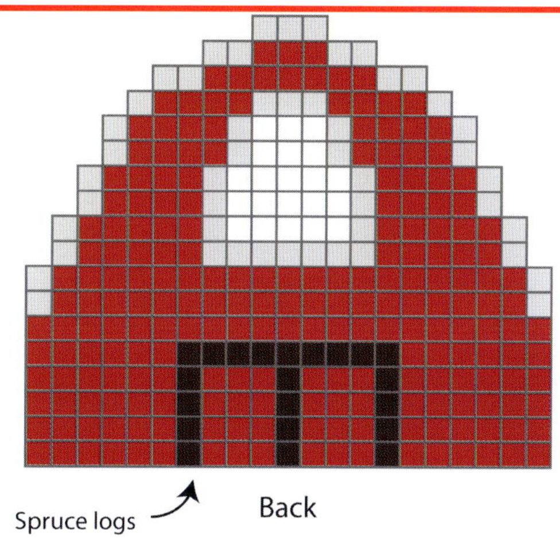

Back

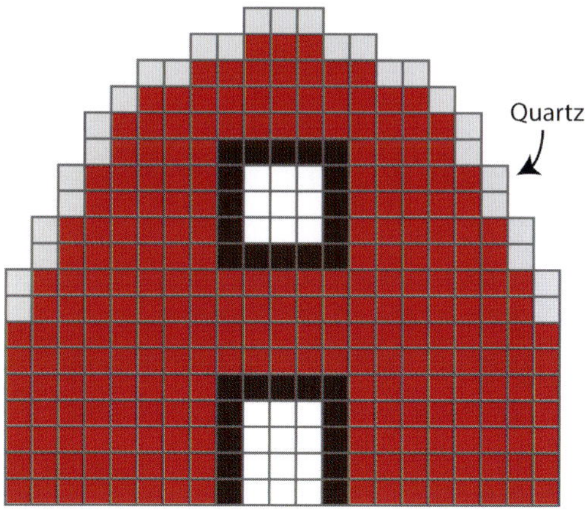

Front

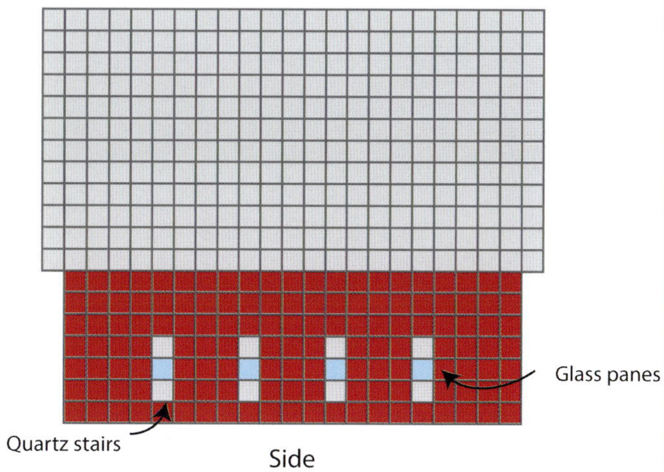

Side

Use the diagram to create the front and back walls. (If you like, you can also use these diagrams to place the front door opening and window and the back window and spruce doorframe. Then you can skip these steps when we get to them.)

Add quartz blocks above the barn roof slope, as shown.

Run these quartz blocks in rows to the back wall. The quartz roof should also extend 1 block beyond the front and back walls.

In the middle of the front wall, break a 5x5 open space. Add spruce blocks to the sides and top of this opening as the barn doorframe.

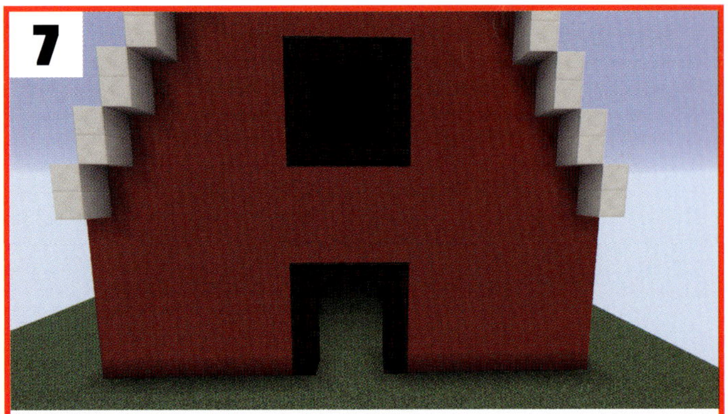

Leave 4 blocks of red terracotta above the door and break another 5x5 hole. Edge this with spruce logs also to create a second floor barn opening.

8

Outside of each of the two front openings, add a door that is 4 blocks wide and 5 high. The outer blocks are quartz, and the inner are red terracotta. Place these so they overlap the openings by 1 block.

9

On the back wall, create the doorframe for a set of closed doors. Break open an entryway 6 blocks high and 9 blocks wide. Add 3 spruce log pillars 6 blocks high to the sides and the center. Add 3 spruce logs at the top of each frame.

10

Leave 3 blocks of terracotta above the doors and create a window of glass panes from 2 rectangles. The bottom rectangle is 5 wide by 3 high, and the top is 3 wide by 2 high.

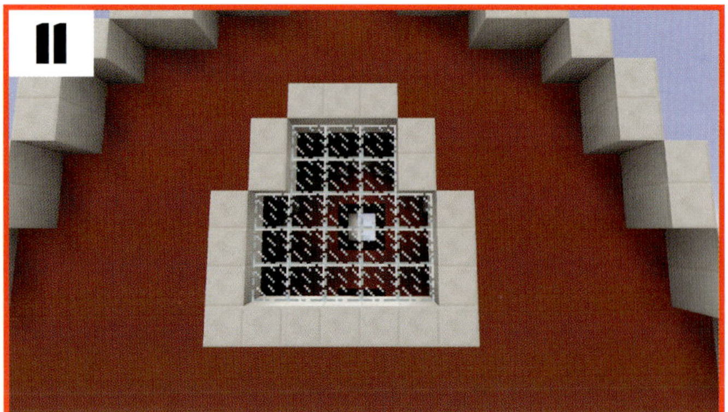

Break blocks to edge this window with quartz.

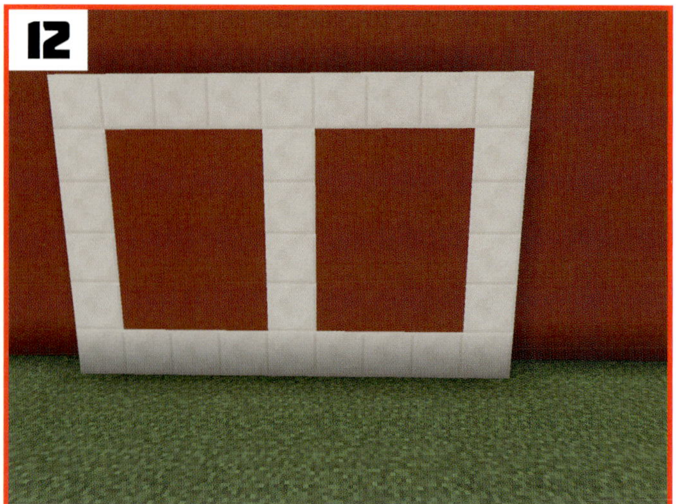

For the bottom doors, place quartz blocks to cover the exposed spruce log frame. Also place quartz blocks at the bottom of the doors. Fill these quartz rectangles in with red terracotta to complete the bottom back doors.

Add 4 side windows to the left and right walls of the barn. Each window is a single glass pane with a quartz stair below and upside-down quartz stair above. Use the diagram to space the 4 windows equally in each side wall.

Inside the barn, add a strip of stone brick flooring, centered, from the front of the barn to the back. Place grass on either side. These 2 strips of grass (or other ground) on each side of the stone bricks are 4 blocks wide.

On top of the left and right sides of the stone brick floor, add a row of spruce wood planks from the front of the barn to the back. These planks will form the front of the stalls.

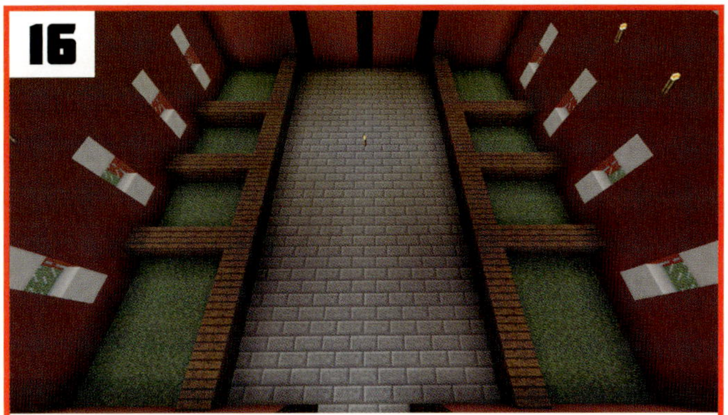

On each side of the barn, divide the space between the stone brick floor and the barn wall into 4 stalls that are 4 blocks deep. The front and back 2 stalls can be 5 wide and the center stalls can be 3 wide.

Add spruce fence gates to the center of the stall front walls and place spruce fences at the top of each stall. Use grass paths as the floor of each stall.

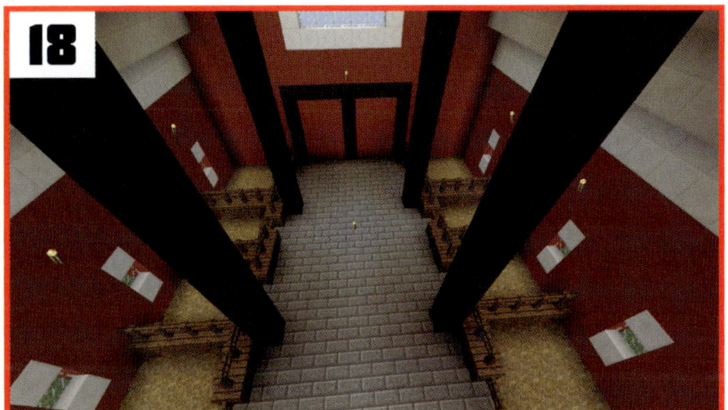

Add 4 spruce log columns just outside the stalls. The front 2 are placed just outside the walls between the 2 front stalls and the next stalls. The back 2 columns are placed outside the walls between the 2 back stalls and the next stalls. Run these columns up to the ceiling.

Add 4 beams of spruce logs that run from the left wall of the barn to the right wall. They should be just below the lowest block of quartz in the roof. Run 2 of the beams against the front and back walls of the barn. Run the middle 2 beams to align with the 4 central pillars.

On top of these beams, add a spruce plank floor. Leave the central portion between the 4 pillars empty.

Add spruce fences around the second floor opening. Add a ladder placed against spruce planks to get up to the floor. Your barn is complete. Move in horses, pigs, sheep, and donkeys, and enjoy. You could even use this barn as a pretty neat home base.

22. LITTLE RED SCHOOLHOUSE

The little, one-room red schoolhouse, whether it's built of bricks or painted red wood, is a classic image of Americana from the 1800s.

All students gathered in the same classroom with usually just one teacher for the whole school. A bell tower was used to ring a bell calling students to class. You can sometimes still find these historical landmarks in the countryside.

MATERIALS

9 stacks bricks
5 stacks stone brick stairs
10 stone bricks
24 stone brick slabs
12 cobblestone walls
14 oak wood planks
22 oak wood stairs
15 oak wood fences
1 oak door
12 wooden pressure plates
20 glass panes
1 iron or gold helmet
1 iron bar
1 armor stand
6 gray wool
12 glowstone blocks
Optional: paintings, item frames, bookshelves, brewing stand, cauldron

Substitutions: Use red concrete or wood planks in place of the bricks.

Clear an area that is about 25x15. Make a 20x11 rectangle of bricks. Persuade any nearby animals to leave the interior of the room.

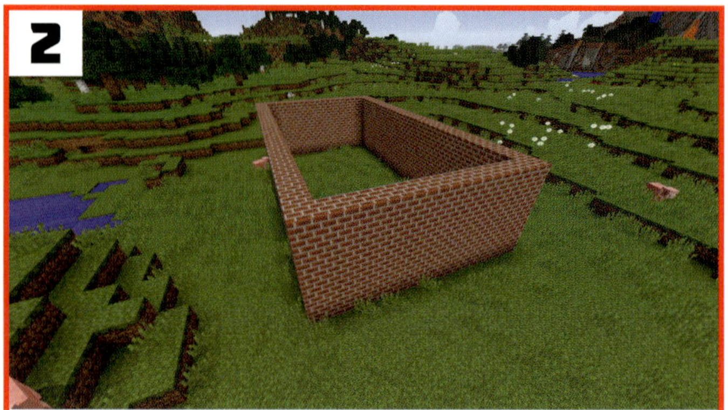

Build the walls of the schoolhouse up to be 5 blocks high.

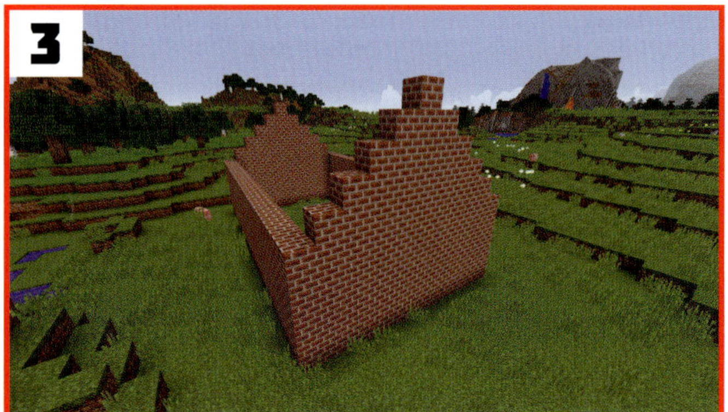

On the front and back walls of the schoolhouse (the short sides), add a triangle of brick blocks. The bottom side of each triangle should be inset 1 block from the side of the schoolhouse. The triangle should be 5 blocks high, with a single brick block at the top.

Now build the roof. Start with rows of stone brick stairs from the front to the back of the schoolhouse. Place them at the same level as the top block of the side wall. They should also extend 1 block out from the front and back walls, as shown.

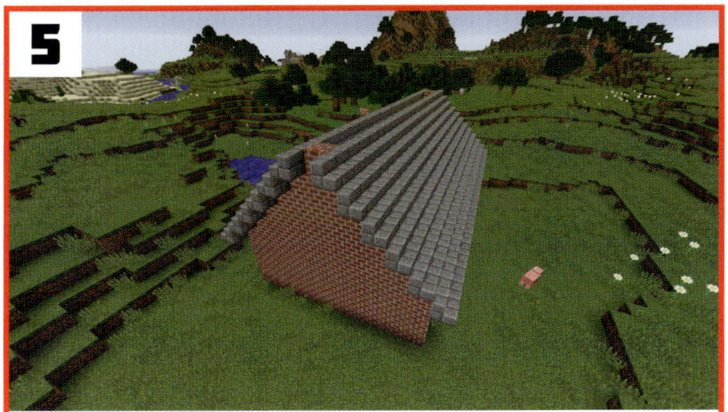

Fill out the roof with rows of stone brick stairs, like the row in step 4, at each level of the triangle except the top.

At the topmost level, place a row of stone brick slabs. Three blocks in from the front of the schoolhouse roof, place a 3x3x3 cube of bricks one block below the top. This is the base of the bell tower.

Now, using bricks, build a wall for the tower that is 1 block tall.

At each corner of the tower, place 2 cobblestone walls.

9

For the base of the tower roof, make a 3x3 square of stone bricks.

10

Above this place a single stone brick block.

11

Encircle the bottom layer of stone bricks with stone brick stairs.

12

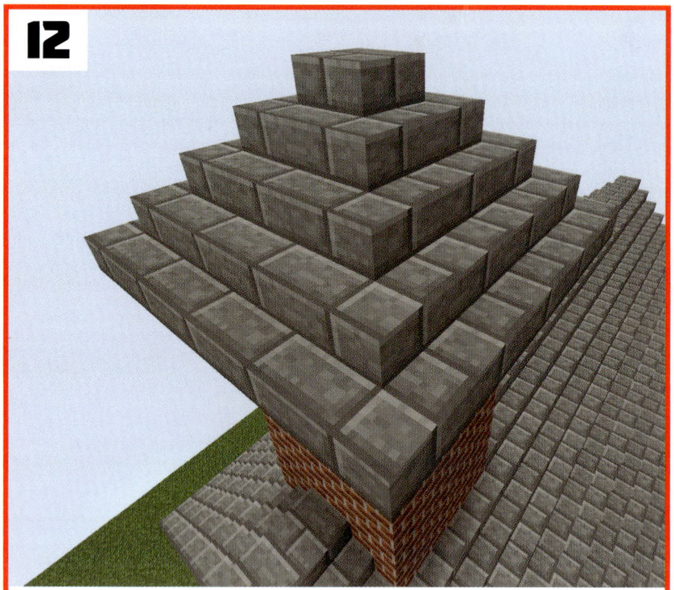

Place stone brick stairs around the top stone brick block to finish the roof.

To make a bell, we're going to use a helmet placed on an armor stand. It won't look like a bell close up, but it will from a distance. First, place an armor stand inside the tower and facing to the back of the school.

Add a gold or iron helmet to the armor stand.

Beneath the roof of the bell tower, in the center, place a single iron bar. This is the rope that holds the bell.

For the school entrance, first build a 3x2 brick rectangle at the center of the front wall.

17

Surround this platform with stone brick stairs.

18

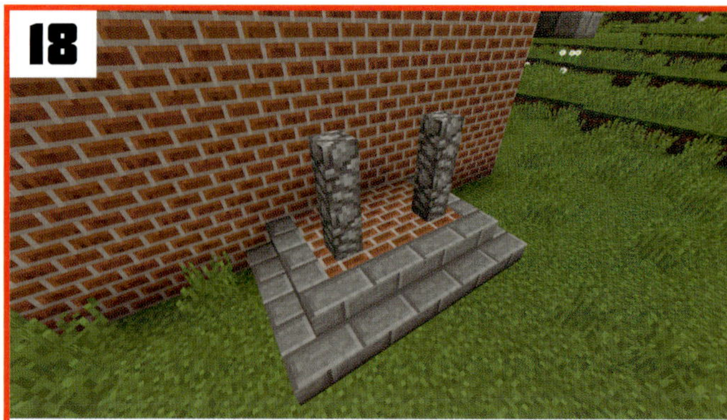

At the 2 front corners of the platform, place cobble walls 2 blocks high.

19

For the entryway roof, place a 2x3 rectangle of stone brick slabs.

20

Place 2 more stone brick slabs for the peak of the entryway roof.

21

Add 3 windows and an oak door to the front of the school, as shown. Use an upside-down stone brick stair as the bottom frame of each window and place 2 glass panes above it.

22

Add 3 more of these windows to the left and right walls of the schoolhouse. Leave 5 blocks of brick before the first window (nearest the front wall). Leave 3 blocks of brick between the first and second windows. Leave 3 blocks of brick between the second and third windows.

23

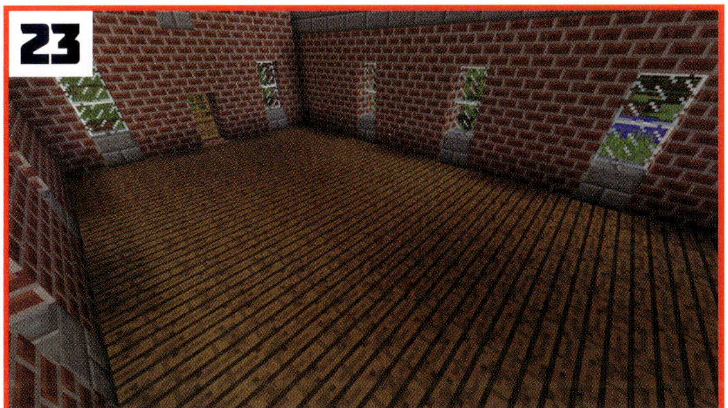

Inside the schoolhouse, add a layer of spruce wood planks for the floor.

24

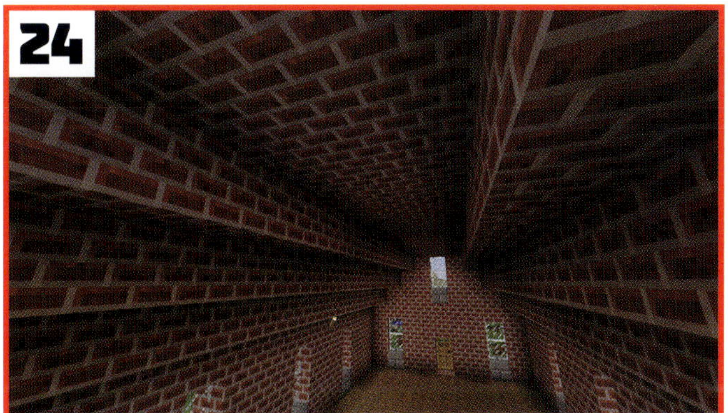

Cover the exposed stone brick roof and the base of the bell tower with brick. Fill in the central, empty row of the inside roof with bricks, as shown.

In the center of the back wall, place a frame of oak wood planks 5 blocks wide and 4 blocks high.

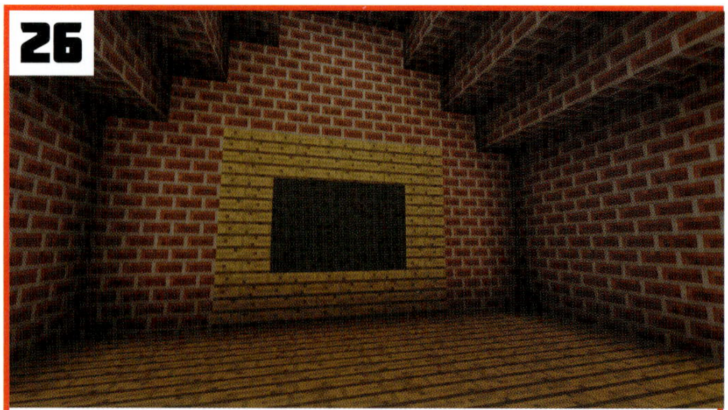

Fill in the frame with gray wool blocks to make a blackboard. Add another layer of bricks to the back wall so it is flush with the blackboard.

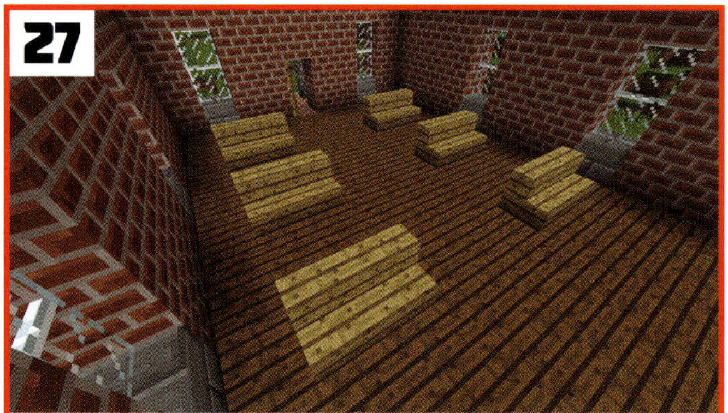

Use oak wood stairs for student seats: 3 rows of 2 seats on each side of the door. Leave 2 blocks of space between each row. Align the back row of desks with the backmost windows.

In front of each seat, add a desk made of an oak fence and a wooden pressure plate.

Add a teacher's desk made of 3 upside-down oak stairs and a chair out of regular oak stairs.

Along the center of the roof, add a row of glowstone blocks for light.

Add your final decorating touches. Add bookshelves, paintings, and item frames with items inside. Add a brewing stand and cauldron for those important potion lessons.

23. CHRISTMAS TREE

Spruce up your Minecraft world with a festive build.

Whether you celebrate Christmas or not, creating a custom tree in Minecraft—and decorating it—can be tons of fun. This tree is decorated in a classic Christmas style, with multicolored ornaments and a star at the top.

MATERIALS

9 stacks spruce leaves
2½ stacks spruce logs
75 colored wool (red, lime green, yellow, orange, magenta, purple)
24 red carpet
32 green carpet
7 glowstones (more if you are adding lights inside the tree)

1

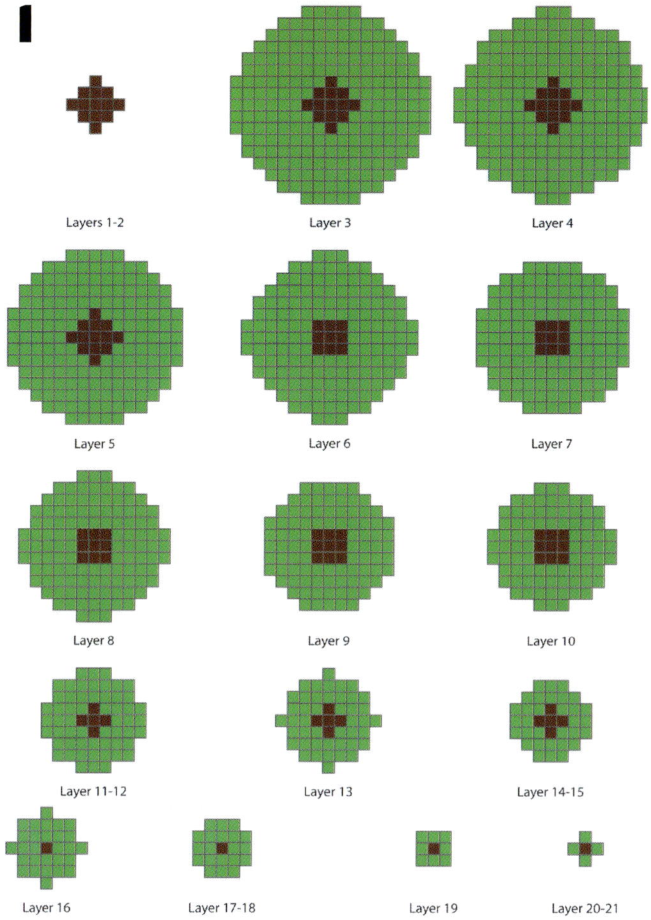

Use the diagram to build up your Christmas tree. The first two brown layers are spruce logs only. After this, brown squares are still spruce logs and green squares are spruce leaf blocks. As you build up the tree, if you want to include lights on the inside of the tree, replace a few of the interior leaf blocks with glowstone blocks every other layer.

2

Once your base tree is finished, add a pillar of 3 glowstone blocks at the very top.

3

Place 4 glowstone blocks around the middle of this pillar to create a star for the tree.

4

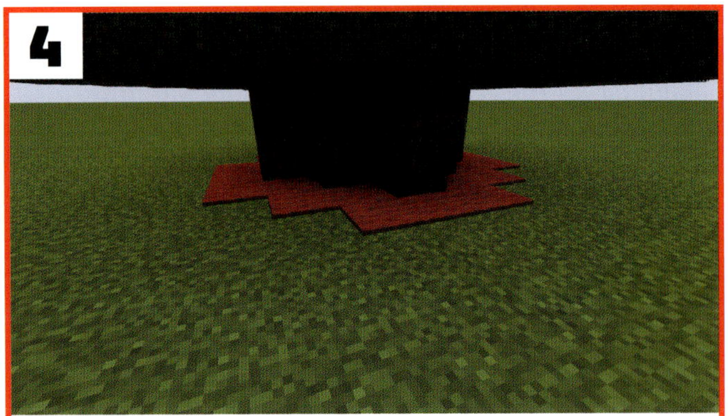

Beneath the tree, use carpet to create Christmas tree skirting. Add a strip of red carpet blocks all around the base of the trunk.

5

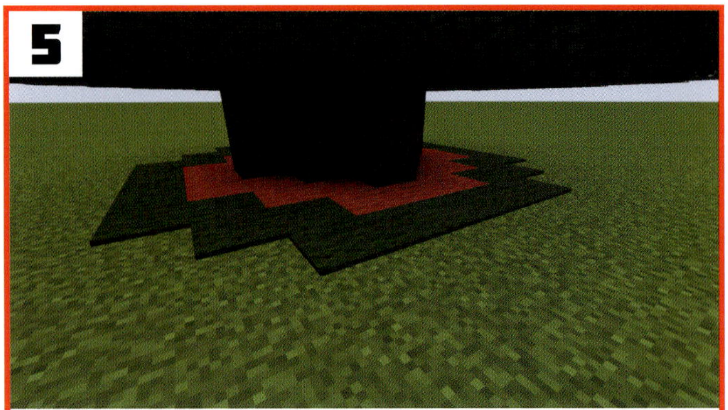

Add a strip of green carpet blocks on the outside of the red carpet, as shown.

6

Finally, use colored wool for tree ornaments. Replace leaf blocks with colored wool and add a few wool blocks on top of leaves.

DID YOU KNOW?

For a couple of days around Christmas, Minecraft chests are changed to look like presents wrapped with ribbons!

24. BRIDGE

If you like to travel in Minecraft by riding your horse, like I do, bridges are a must.

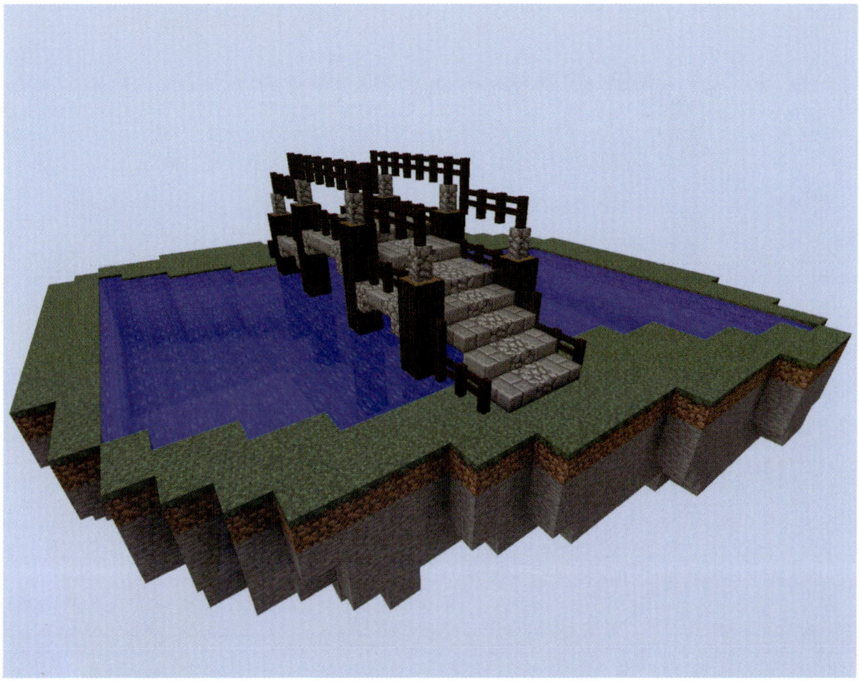

Horses will throw you off if you get into water more than a couple blocks deep for more than a moment. Although a quick solution is just to place wood planks across a river, it's awfully nice to have a good-looking bridge. Here's one that you can easily make longer or shorter by changing the length of the middle section.

MATERIALS

70 spruce wood logs
48 stone brick slabs
20 cobblestone slabs
68 dark oak wood fences
8 cobblestone walls
12 cobblestone stairs

Substitutions: Use different wood in place of the spruce wood logs and dark wood fences.

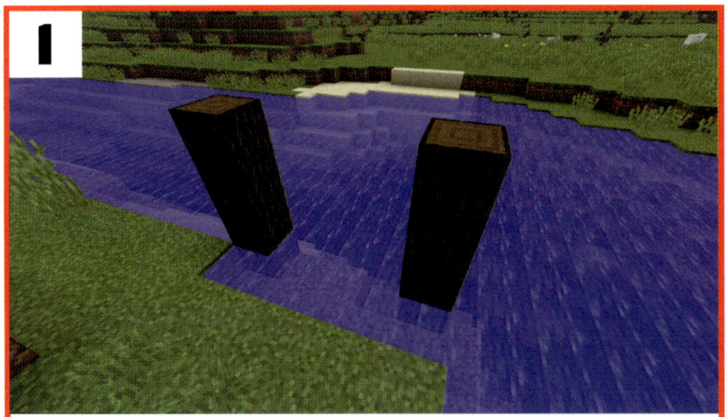

On one side of the river place 2 piers, or supporting pillars, for the bridge. Use spruce wood logs and place them 2 blocks into the river, as shown. They should be 4 blocks apart from each other, leaving 3 empty blocks between them. They should reach all the way down to the river's bottom and extend out of the water 3 blocks.

Between the 2 piers, 1 block down from the top, add a row of 3 slabs: stone brick slabs on the outside and 1 cobblestone slab in the middle.

Do the same on the other side of the river. Make sure these 2 piers line up with the first ones you built.

Four blocks from the existing piers, place another 2 sets of piers further into the river. These should extend 4 blocks out of the water and leave 3 empty blocks between them and the piers placed in steps 1 and 3.

One block down from the top of the inner piers, add 2 rows of slabs like the rows placed in step 2. Do this on both sides of the bridge.

Between the 2 sets of inner piers, add 4 rows of slabs a half block higher than those you've already placed, as shown.

Between the outer and inner slabs, add 2 rows of slabs a half block higher than the outer slabs. Do this on both sides of the bridge.

Add 3 more rows of slabs extending from the outermost piers.The rows should descend a half block with each row to reach the bank. Do this on both sides of the bridge.

On each side of the bridge, between the sets of piers, place pairs of upside-down cobblestone stairs facing each other.

Add stone brick slabs between the pairs of stairs.

Place dark oak fences all along the stairs and slabs you placed in steps 9 and 10.

Place dark oak fences on the outer portions of the bridge, as shown.

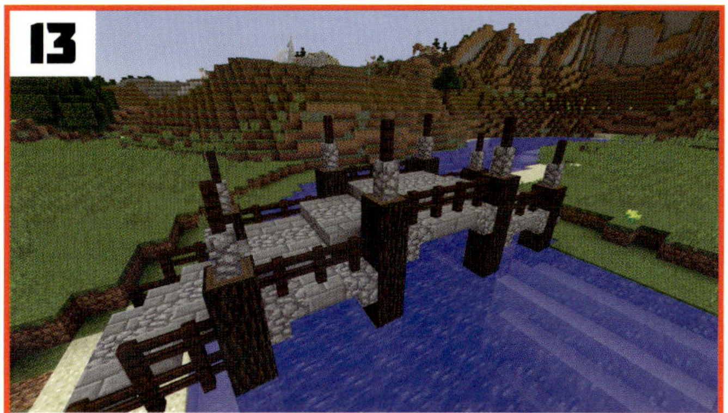

Place a cobblestone wall on top of each pier and on top of these dark oak fences.

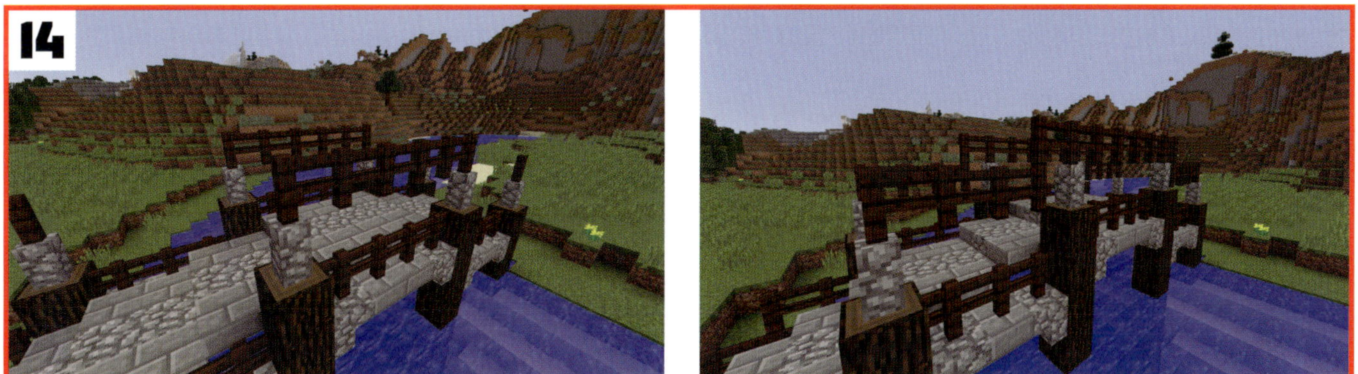

Connect these fences together with more dark oak fences, as shown.

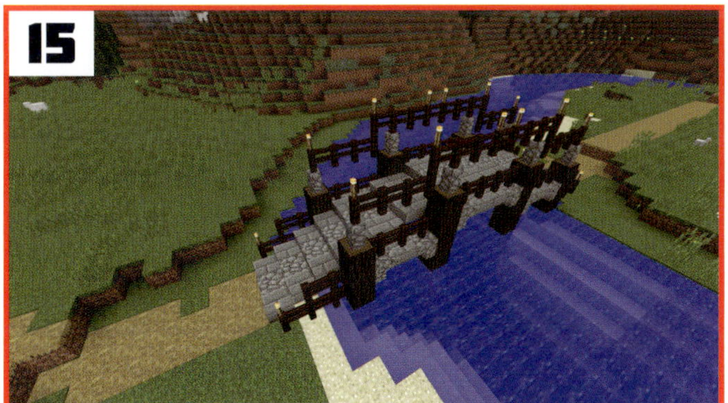

Your bridge is done! Add lights and roads or paths leading to the bridge as you like.

25. COZY CASTLE

Here's a castle that's a standout but won't take you forever to build because of its manageable size.

This small castle is based very loosely on the gatehouse of a real abbey in England called Alnwick Abbey. This home has the benefit of being a castle, with towers and crenellations, but it's also a comfortable and cozy size.

MATERIALS

17½ stacks stone bricks
10 stone brick stairs
1 stack cobblestone
4½ stacks cobblestone stairs
6½ stacks spruce wood planks
2½ stacks spruce logs
48 dark oak fences
18 spruce doors

Clear out an area that is about 24 blocks square. First you'll build the towers. They are each a 5x5 square. The right towers are 8 blocks away from the left (leaving 7 empty blocks between them). The back towers are 6 blocks away from the front towers (leaving 5 empty blocks between). The towers are made of stone brick, and the 3 outer corners of each tower are made of spruce logs.

Build these towers up to be 14 blocks high.

Inside each tower, 1 block below the top of the 4 walls, add a floor made of spruce wood planks.

Add upside-down cobblestone stairs all the way around the towers, 1 block down from the top.

At each corner of each tower, above the cobblestone stairs, add a column of 3 cobblestone blocks.

Between these cobblestone pillars on each side of each tower, add a row of spruce logs.

Above the spruce logs, place rows of stone bricks that are 1 block high.

Above the rows of stone bricks, add 2 more stone brick blocks, as shown, to finish the castle crenellations.

On the left and right sides of the castle, add a stone brick wall 1 block in from the tower walls. Build up this wall to be 15 blocks high.

At the back of the castle, add a stone brick wall 1 block in from the tower walls. Build it up to be 12 blocks high.

On top of this wall, break the 2 cobblestone stairs on the tower walls on either side. Add 4 cobblestone blocks, as shown, for crenellations.

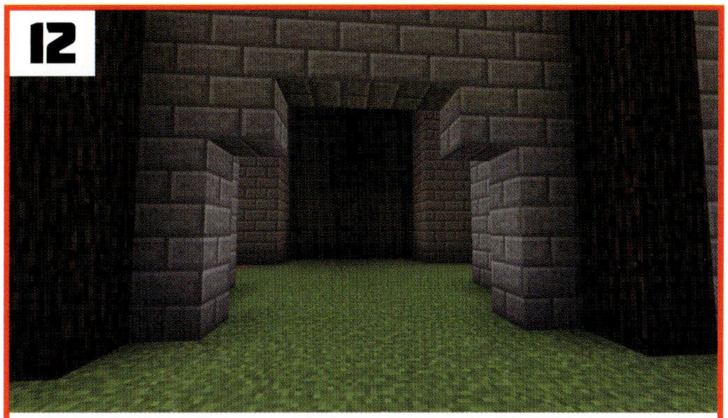

At the front of the castle, build a similar wall at the front that is 12 blocks high and 1 block indented from the front tower walls. However, at the bottom, leave an arched opening that is 4 blocks high, as shown. The top of the arch leaves 3 blocks of space, and the bottom leaves 5 blocks of space.

At the top of the front wall, place a row of upside-down cobblestone stairs.

On top of these stairs, add a row of stone bricks.

15

Above this row, place 2 stone brick blocks as crenellations.

16

Just inside the entryway, add a row of stone bricks from the left tower to the right, as shown.

17

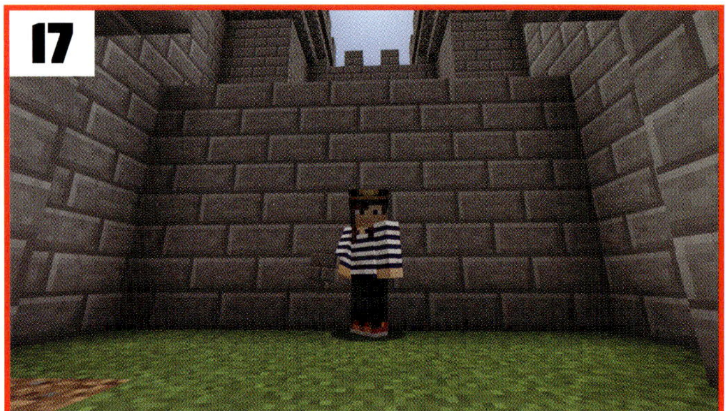

Build this row up as a wall 4 blocks high.

18

Add a spruce door to the center of this wall, and add cobblestone as the floor for the entryway.

19

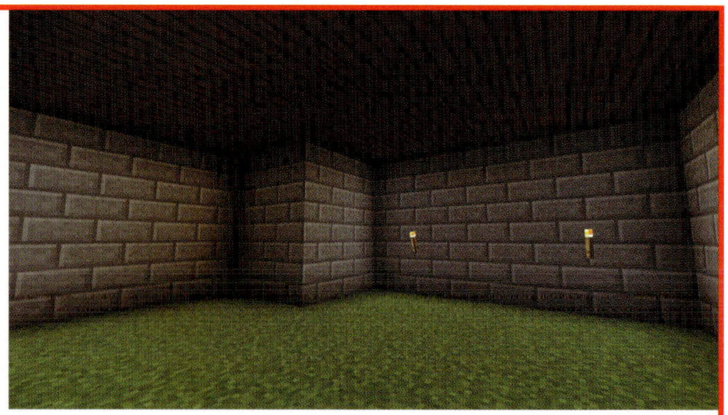

Inside the castle, add a spruce plank floor right above the entryway wall you built in step 15.

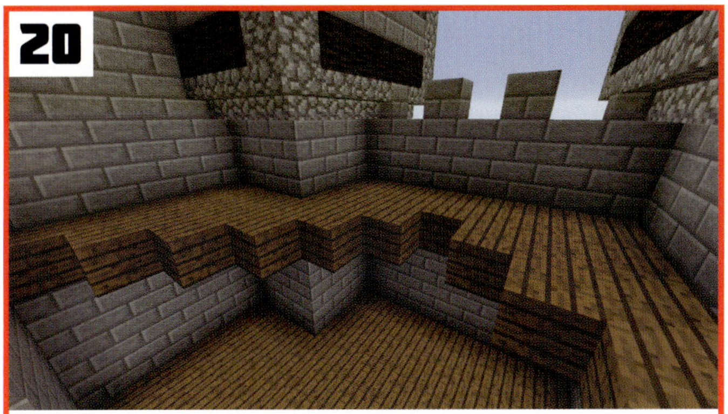

20

Five blocks above the first floor (leaving 4 empty blocks between), build another spruce plank floor (but fill the floor in all the way).

21

Now that the structure is pretty much complete, we can detail the castle. First, add a row of cobblestone staircase all around the castle's outside wall on the ground. One block above the top of the entryway, add a row of upside-down cobblestone stairs. These stairs should also go around the whole castle.

22

Add dark oak fences and a stone brick floor to the entryway, as shown.

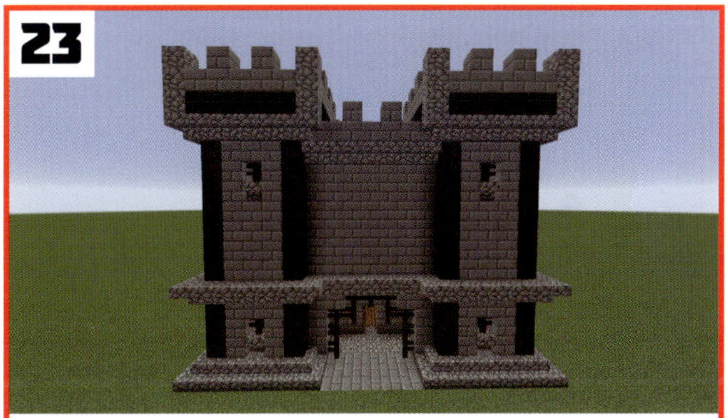

23

On each of the 4 towers' 2 outside walls, add 2 windows. The windows are made of 1 dark oak fence and 1 upside-down cobblestone stair. Place lower windows 2 blocks down from the middle row of cobblestone stairs. Place the upper windows 2 blocks down from the upper row of cobble stone stairs.

24

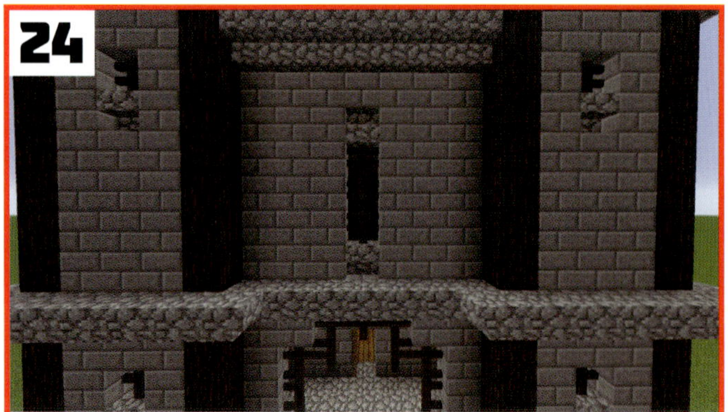

In the front, central wall of the castle, add a tall window using 3 dark oak fences. Place an upside-down cobblestone stair at the bottom of the window and a regular cobblestone stair at the top.

25

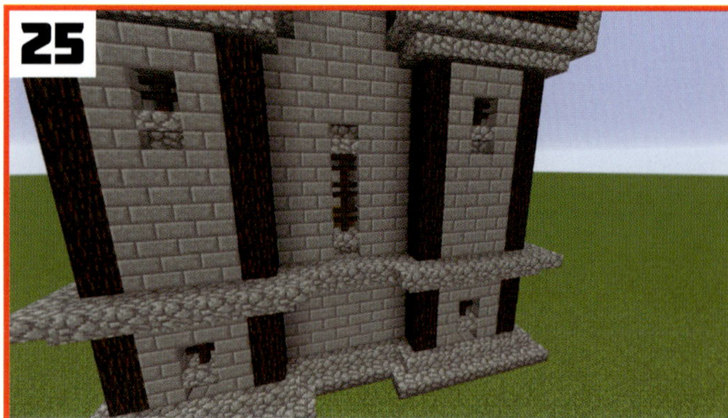

Add identical windows to the sides and back of the castle.

26

At the back of the castle, add 3 windows, each made of 3 dark oak fences, as shown.

27

On the left and right sides of the castle, add a row of spruce logs between the 2 towers, as shown.

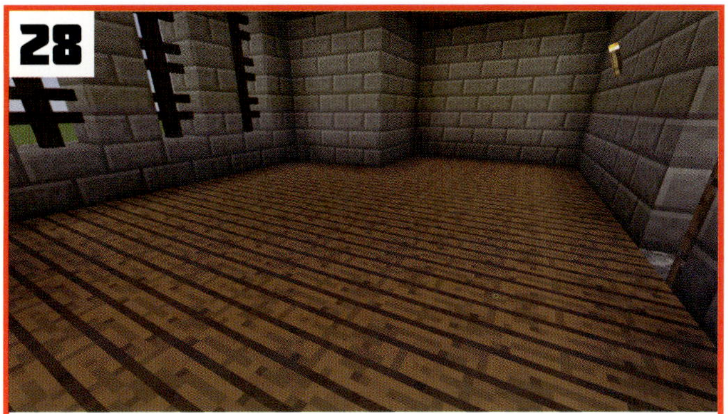

Inside the castle, add spruce planks for the floor.

On the right side of the ground floor, add stone brick staircases to the second floor. Use spruce wood planks as the staircase base and stone brick stairs, as shown.

Do the same for the left side of the castle.

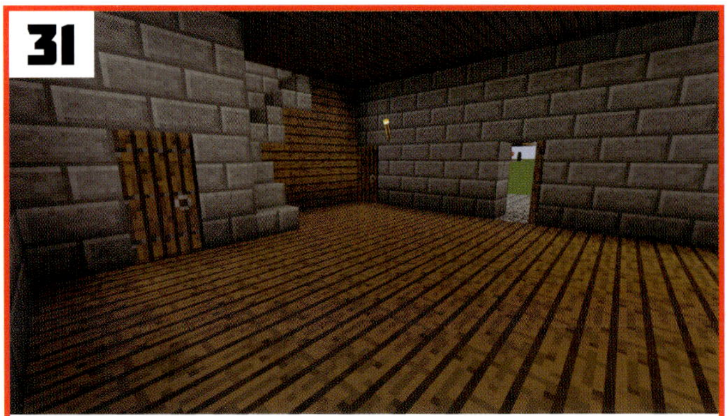

Add spruce doors leading to the 4 towers on the ground floor and make the tower floors out of spruce wood planks.

On the second floor, add 4 more doors to enter the towers and add floors of spruce wood planks.

On the castle roof, add doors to the towers and spruce floors. Add ladders to 1 or more of the towers so that you can reach the castle roof from the second floor as well as the tower roofs. You're ready to move into your castle now and add your bed, chests, decorations, and landscaping.